Slowly, slowly, hardly daring to look, Mari lifted her head and pushed herself to a standing position.

Just in time to see a tall sailor step off his boat onto the jetty, coil the rope around a bollard on the pontoon one-handed and use his other hand to rake his fingers from his forehead back through his hair, as if the wind had made a nuisance of itself by messing up his hairstyle.

The sail was down and neatly wrapped, the boat was perfectly aligned in a berth in calm waters and the sailor looked so composed he might have just stepped from a cruise ship on a lazy summer afternoon.

Stunned and totally bewildered, Mari could only watch in amazed silence as the tall man double-checked the rope, glanced at his watch and then turned around to stroll casually away from her, down the walkway that led back to the town. And just for a second she saw his face for the first time.

Her heart missed a beat.

Ethan Chandler was back in town.

Dear Reader,

Given the choice, I would love to spend each and every summer by the sea, preferably accompanied by a sandy beach, hot sunshine and a suitcase of great books. Over the years, some of my favorite holidays have been spent on small Greek Islands where the evening entertainment consisted of watching boats of all sizes—from luxury yachts to three-masted wooden sailing ships—sailing into harbour for the night. Some are pleasure craft, but many are oceangoing yachts crewed by men and women who have chosen a life at sea.

Ethan Chandler is a professional yachtsman who has been sailing away from his loss and pain for the past ten years. Now he has returned to the small Dorset coastal town where his career began. And to the girl he left behind. Both of them have had to brave stormy waters to make their way in life, but can they stop running away long enough to find happiness?

I do hope that you enjoy Ethan and Mari's journey to love and the happiness that they each deserve. I am always delighted to hear from my readers, and you can get in touch via my website, www.NinaHarrington.com.

Every best wish,

Nina

NINA HARRINGTON
Blind Date Rivals

TORONTO NEW YORK LONDON
AMSTERDAM PARIS SYDNEY HAMBURG
STOCKHOLM ATHENS TOKYO MILAN MADRID
PRAGUE WARSAW BUDAPEST AUCKLAND

Recycling programs
for this product may
not exist in your area.

ISBN-13: 978-0-373-74135-9

BLIND DATE RIVALS

First North American Publication 2011

Nina Harrington grew up in rural Northumberland, England, and decided at the age of eleven that she was going to be a librarian—because then she could read *all* of the books in the public library whenever she wanted! Since then she has been a shop assistant, community pharmacist, technical writer, university lecturer, volcano walker and industrial scientist, before taking a career break to realise her dream of being a fiction writer. When she is not creating stories that make her readers smile, her hobbies are cooking, eating, enjoying good wine—and talking, for which she has had specialist training.

CHAPTER ONE

'WELL, good afternoon. Have I reached the offices of one Sara Jane Fenchurch? The same Sara Jane Fenchurch who is shortlisted to be the next local Businesswoman of the Year? I have *Orchid Growers Monthly* waiting on line two for an exclusive interview. Could that be you, Miss Fenchurch? Hiding behind the smuggest grin in the potting shed?'

Sara sat back in the chair she had rescued from a skip two weeks earlier and twirled her pen between two fingers like a cheerleader. Her best friend, Helen, waltzed into the cramped office on crazily high heels, whisked dirt from an old dining room chair with a perfectly manicured hand and perched elegantly on the edge of the hard seat.

'Oh?' Sara replied, wide-eyed in pretend amazement, and pressed the fingertips of her left hand to her chest. 'Could that be little old me?' And then she fluttered her eyelashes dramatically towards a framed newspaper cutting which dominated the plain wall of the log cabin which had been a potting shed but was now her garden office. A photographer from the local free newspaper had caught her grinning like a loon and looking as stunned as a rabbit caught in car headlights as the organiser congratulated her for being on the shortlist. 'Why, yes, I believe it is. Fancy that. Maybe this year I will win it? That would be nice. Not to say useful. Cottage Orchids needs as much publicity as it can get, thank you.'

Helen snorted derisively and brushed away a trail of cobweb from the skirt of her otherwise immaculate burgundy bouclé suit. 'Of course you'll win and your orchids will be positively flying out of the door. Although...' and Helen raised her eyebrows and tilted her head to one side as she looked at Sara from head to toe before tutting loudly '...you are going to need a serious makeover, young lady, if you want to impress those judges. We can start by getting rid of that hideous pen.'

Helen tried to snatch Sara's favourite pen from between her friend's fingers, but Sara was too quick for her and lifted it out of reach behind her head.

'There is nothing wrong with my pen,' Sara replied indignantly. 'Leave it alone.'

'It's green and sparkly with a bendy plastic flower stuck on the top. Not very professional, is it?'

'It came free with a bag of orchid compost and I like it and it writes,' Sara replied. 'Professional pens are for girls who have money to spend on luxuries. Not girls who need to save every penny to invest in their orchid houses.'

Helen sighed out loud and shook her head. 'A green flowery pen. What would the Dragon have said?' Then she grinned across at Sara, pressed the back of her hand to her forehead and went on in a thin, high, whiny voice of horror, 'How inelegant, my dears. *The shame.*'

Sara laughed out loud, pushed the pointy end of her green pen behind her ear so that the yellow flower bobbed up and down at Helen, and leant her elbows on top of the pile of papers stacked several inches thick on the pine kitchen table which served as her office desk. The headmistress at the private boarding school where Sara had first met Helen had been a former actress and was famous for seizing on every opportunity for an over the top dramatic performance. Helen had always been able to mimic her perfectly.

'Maybe you are right, but at least one of us didn't let her down on the elegance front.' Then Sara brightened and looked at Helen through narrowed eyes. 'You look far too chirpy for a girl who is celebrating being a year older. In fact, if I didn't know you better I would have said you were scheming about something. Let me guess. You've changed your mind about celebrating your birthday here in the quaint little English village I call home and are planning to fly off to some exotic paradise with your beloved Caspar instead?'

'Are you kidding? I've loved this place since the very first time your lovely nana took pity on me during the school holidays.' Then Helen smiled and gave Sara that certain innocent look that made Sara's eyebrows lift. 'Actually, this time it's more along the lines of what I can do for you!'

Helen leant forward and flashed her expensive dentistry for a second in a wide grin. 'It took some doing, but Caspar finally managed to persuade his friend Leo to leave London early so that he can come along to my birthday party at the hotel tonight! Isn't that wonderful news?'

Sara shook her head very slowly from side to side. 'Oh, no. You are not doing this to me. Not again. Just because I'm single does not mean that you have to try and set me up with every single, divorced or otherwise unattached man within a hundred mile radius.'

Helen sighed in exasperation. 'But he is perfect for you. Just think of it as a small thank you for offering to do the wedding flowers! Besides, Caspar doesn't have many close friends and at this rate Leo Grainger is going to be the only single usher at my wedding! Come on, I hate the idea that I'm the first of us to be getting married and you don't even have a boyfriend who I can torment. Who knows? You might actually like him and enjoy yourself?'

Sara picked up a bulging document folder from her desk and let it fall back with a thud, causing the withered elastic band that was holding it together to give up and twang into shreds. 'It's a good thing that your wedding isn't for another four weeks! Seriously, Helen, I'm swamped with paperwork and there is so much still to do I'm dizzy. *And* I have to be up on time tomorrow to meet the Events Manager at the Manor. There is no room in my life for dating. And you might recall that my last boyfriend was not a huge success.'

Helen waved her fingers in the air and coughed. 'That was three years ago and I thought we promised to never talk about that loser again. Don't waste one second even thinking about how he let you down.'

Sara pushed her lips together. 'Let me down? Is that what you call breaking up with me and running off to Australia with his office junior?

No, Gorgeous. I love you and you have been my best friend since the first time we shared homesick stories aged eight, but no boyfriends. Thank you all the same but I am sure that Caspar's friend will have a great time at the party without me boring him to tears with talk of orchid fertiliser.'

Helen glanced around the wooden walls, shivered and sniffed dramatically and dropped her voice down to a pleading whisper. 'Fair point. Except, you know this could be the last time we go out partying together as single girls, don't you? In only a few weeks' time, I am going to be Mrs Caspar Kaplinski. I shall *try* to understand that you are so busy in your own life that you can't spare a *few* hours to help your old friend celebrate her last birthday as a single girl. Although it is going to be quite a struggle. I...I don't know if I can go through with it knowing that my one and only bridesmaid is going to be sitting in her tiny hovel all evening. Lonely and rejected while we are all enjoying ourselves...'

Her voice tailed off with a dramatic over the top fake sob, and she pressed a real silk handkerchief to the inner corner of each eye.

'That. Is emotional blackmail. And my cottage is not a hovel. Yesterday you called it a bijou gem!'

'Absolutely!' Helen replied with a wide grin,

already on her feet and heading for the door. 'So, it's decided then. Cinders, you shall not stay home with only your elderly cat for company. Not this Saturday night. I shall slip through the back gate to collect you at eight with the props and stuff. Leo will take one look at you and be totally smitten, you wait and see. This is one party you're going to remember. Ciao.'

'Props? Helen! Wait!'

Sara stared at the space where her best friend had been sitting. How did Helen do it? A costume party *and* a blind date? Sara pressed her eyes tight shut and slumped back in her chair. *Oh, no.* She had a horrible feeling that she was going to regret this.

'Leo, my old mate,' Caspar bellowed down Leo's car telephone system, 'where are you? Helen is starting to panic that you've run away in terror at the thought of meeting your blind date this evening. You have to help me out here.'

'Me? Run away from a gorgeous lady? Perish the thought.' Then there was a pause before Leo asked, 'She isn't another of Helen's old school friends, is she?'

The less than reassuring silence on the other end of the telephone confirmed his worst fears. 'Ah, well,' Caspar answered. 'This one is different! Sara might be a country girl but she is very sweet.'

'A country girl?' Leo laughed. 'You do remember you are talking to a city boy? London born and bred. I don't do country. I have no idea why Helen thinks I'm in desperate need of female company. Perhaps she has a secret yearning to change direction and set up shop as a matchmaker?'

'That's my girl!' Caspar snorted. 'Always looking out for her friends. Anyway. Any idea what time you might be arriving? I need to get your costume ready.'

Leo checked his car navigation display. 'Apparently I should be with you in about ten minutes. In fact I've just turned into Kingsmede and seen the sign for the hotel. Kingsmede Manor, here I come.' And then he paused, distracted for a moment by another car. 'Did you just use the word costume? *Caspar?*'

'Brilliant! Ring me when you're settled. I owe you a drink.'

And, with that, Caspar's voice closed off, leaving Leo to the luxury of the hum of the powerful engine as the car made its way down the country lanes of the sleepy English countryside on a warm Saturday evening.

A blind date! And of course Caspar had only informed him about that small detail when he was already halfway to the middle of nowhere! Helen had a heart of gold but the last thing he wanted at this precise moment in his life was a blind date, or any date at all for that matter. He already had more than enough on his plate at the moment.

Of course he would be polite, and he was grateful for the rare chance to enjoy himself with Caspar and celebrate Helen's birthday but the rest of this weekend was going to be work!

He felt guilty about not telling Caspar the truth but his aunt Arabella had made it clear that she did not want anyone to know that she had hired Grainger Consulting to work on a very special project. Her company had bought Kingsmede Manor three years ago and invested heavily to restore it.

Now she was determined to leverage the asset and maximise the returns to justify that investment.

The latest idea from the management team was to buy the land next to the hotel and build a luxury spa extension. But Arabella wanted a second opinion—*his opinion*—before they gave the spa idea the final go-ahead.

Normally he would have sent one of his team along to do the work, but not this time. He owed his aunt more than he could ever repay. And for that he was willing to take time away from the

London office and do the work himself as a personal favour, when he could least afford to. His workload over the past few months had been hectic.

Worse. He had a deadline. And it was tight. He had to come up with something very, very special in five days. The entire board of directors of Rizzi Hotels would be meeting at Kingsmede Manor over lunch on Friday for their annual general meeting.

Nothing so unusual about that.

Companies paid Grainger Consulting to make the hard decisions about what they needed to do to survive in hard times, and he had built his reputation on doing precisely that. But this time it was personal.

Leo's fingers wrapped tight around the steering wheel.

The Rizzi Hotel chain owned some of the most prestigious boutique hotels around the world, but it was still a family business, with one domineering and driven man at the top—his own grandfather. Paolo Leonardo Rizzi. The man he despised for his uncaring ruthlessness. The man who expected his orders to be obeyed by everyone, and especially by his own family.

There was no room for sentiment or consideration of the human costs to the hotels they bought out in Paolo Rizzi's world.

Of course Arabella knew that he would create something outstanding to present to the family on Friday. Clever, shrewd and powerful, his aunt was giving him the chance to settle the score with the grandfather who had so fundamentally rejected his own daughter and her family.

And Leo was determined to prove just how big a mistake that had been.

All he had to do was to create a stunning proposal on how to make Kingsmede Manor Hotel more profitable, and keep the project secret for the next few days. *Nothing to it.*

Leo Grainger eased his foot off the accelerator and turned slowly into the long paved drive that led to the hotel. Each side of the drive was lined with full-size beech trees with branches so high and wide that they joined in the middle to create a tunnel of soft green leaves, shading the drivers from the June sunshine. At eight in the evening, the shadows and sunlight created a dazzling display on the windscreen of his sports car.

These tree-lined avenues had been created centuries ago to impress guests arriving at the house for the first time in horse-drawn carriages. According to the dossier his aunt had sent over, Kingsmede Manor had been a private house until only three years earlier and had actually remained in the same family since the time it was built.

That had to be a useful selling point. Overseas visitors adored English heritage—especially when it was as eccentric as this.

Coming out of the shadows and into the low sunlight of the summer evening, Leo squinted through the windscreen and took his first sight of the house. The drive in front of the house turned into a wide circle around a central fountain where a swan frolicked in the cascading spray.

A brief smile flashed across his lips. *Impressive.* No wonder his aunt had snapped the house up the minute it came onto the market. She had impeccable taste.

Minutes later, Leo threw open the car door, swung his body out of the bucket seat and stepped out onto the cobblestone car park. His favourite designer black boots emerged first, followed by the rest of him, all six foot two of gym-toned muscle, sharp reflexes and an uncanny instinct for what made a commercial business a success...or at least that was what the financial press liked to say.

In his high-profile work with international clients, superficial aspects such as his designer clothing were simply parts of a business image he had spent years perfecting. His clients expected prestige and results and that was what they got. It was as simple as that. They did not care that he had started his working life washing dishes in the kitchens of his aunt's boutique London hotel. Why should they? He was paid to make a difference to their business. Nothing else mattered. This was business, not personal.

And now it was time to do the same for Kingsmede Manor.

Leo strolled around to the back of the car and lifted out his leather weekend bag. His only hope was that there would be a marked absence of those boring white orchids that every hotel in the world seemed to have at the moment. Perhaps this time he was going to get a pleasant surprise?

It was almost nine that evening when Sara finally tottered in her evening sandals through the familiar white marble hall with its twisted double staircase and grinned up at the huge scarlet banner which hung suspended from the ornate plasterwork arch above her head.

The words 'Hollywood Night' had been printed in enormous gold letters across the banner. Trust Helen to choose a movie theme for her birthday party. And subtle did not come into it.

Shaking her head with a low chuckle, Sara

could not resist checking on the pair of stunning orchid plants which she had delivered only two days earlier as a special order.

This variety of Phalaenopsis was a triumph. At the heart of each of the huge ivory blossoms was a crimson tongue speckled with gold dust. Of course she did not expect the guests and staff at the hotel to appreciate how much work went into create such perfect flower spikes from each plant, but they did look amazing. She had suggested other colour combinations, of course, but the Events Manager had insisted on the ivory blossoms. They were a lovely match for the antique console table which stood along the length of the hall below the huge gold framed mirror which had once belonged to her grandmother.

It had been heartbreaking for her to watch so many of her favourite pieces of treasured antique furniture being sold off in auction to strangers, but her mother had been right for once. Huge heavy pieces of furniture and enormous gilt mirrors belonged in a house large enough to appreciate them and not in some minimalist apartment or tiny cottage. And of course they had needed the proceeds of the sale so very badly.

At least the luxury hotel chain who had bought Kingsmede Manor had the good sense to snap up as many of the lovely original pieces as they could while they still had the chance.

At that moment the front doors opened to a gaggle of laughing guests who swept into the hall, bringing a breeze of evening air to waft through the orchid spikes. Sara did not recognise anyone in the group—but that was hardly surprising. Helen's jewellery design business was based in London and it had been three years since they had shared a flat together. Their lives had changed so much since then it was little wonder that they had different friends and such different lives.

For a moment Sara looked past the orchid blossoms and caught her reflection in the mirror. Her hand instantly went to her hair and flicked back her short fringe. There had been a time when she had been one of those laughing, happy city girls, with their smart high heels and expensive grooming habits, who could afford wonderful hairdressers. Now she was simply grateful that the pixie style was back in fashion.

Sara checked her watch. She was late. Correction, make that *very late*. Perhaps her blind date was already here and waiting for her? Frightened of being stood up? And probably as scared as she was.

She lifted her chin and fixed a smile on her lips as she wandered into what had been her grandmother's drawing room and stood on tiptoe to see if she could spot Helen.

At five feet nothing, Helen had always been petite enough to make Sara feel like a gangly beanstalk. That was one reason why Sara had chosen medium black sandals to accompany her simple black shift dress—one of the many treasures her grandmother had left behind in the dressing-up box! Helen had supplied the pearl necklaces and huge black sunglasses but she had turned down the plastic tiara. Not with her current hairstyle. The long black evening gloves and cigarette-holder were the only other props she needed to become Audrey for the evening.

Then she spotted someone waving to her from across the room.

Sara worked her way through the crowd of costumed strangers, trying to reach Helen's table which was just in front of the wide patio doors that led out onto the terrace. A warm breeze from the garden wafted into the packed room. Perfect.

'Thank goodness you are here,' Helen called against the background noise. 'We need to come up with a plan to make sure that we win the karaoke contest later on, and you're the only person I know who can sing vaguely in tune.'

Helen was dressed as Dorothy in *The Wizard of Oz* and looked absolutely charming, from her simple gingham pinafore dress to her red glittery shoes and a tiny little basket with a stuffed toy dog inside.

'Oh, thanks a lot, Dotty,' Sara replied with a laugh and bent down quickly to kiss her friend, while trying to avoid kissing away the bright spot of red on Helen's cheek which she had helped apply. 'Sorry I'm so late. I think the mice have been in the orchid house again and Pasha refused to move from his comfy cat bed without a fight.'

Sara stretched out her left arm and turned it from side to side. 'Can you still see the scratch marks? I've taken two antihistamines and tried to cover them up with several layers of make-up and long gloves. What do you think?'

Helen waved her fingers in the air. 'Forget about all of that. I need you to focus, sweetie. Focus. I have just decided that our table will win the most points so you have to be on top form.' She nodded and tapped her finger against her nose, which was slightly redder than normal, and Sara wondered how many glasses of champagne Helen had sampled in the past hour.

But, before Sara could answer, a tall slim man in a pinstriped suit with huge shoulders, black and white brogues, a fedora and black eye mask sidled up towards them, tipped his hat to an even more jaunty angle, lifted Helen's hand, bent over sharply from the waist and kissed the inside of her wrist. 'Hiya, Gorgeous,' he said in a very fake American gangster accent, 'are you ready to be my moll tonight? You and your little dog too.'

'Good evening, Caspar,' Sara said with a smile. 'You are looking terribly elegant.'

The black silk mask was hoisted up with a sigh of exasperation.

'Come on. What gave me away?' Caspar asked.

Sara pointed to his wrist. 'I'm afraid designer watches like that were not so very common in the organised crime community.'

He looked casually down and snorted. 'Serves me right for accepting gifts from every jewellery designer I promise to marry,' he answered, grinning down at Helen, who raised her eyebrows in recognition.

'Anyway—look at you! All dressed up for a Saturday night and looking very handsome.'

'Helen dragged me here.' Sara nodded. 'Apparently this is the poor girl's last chance to have some fun before she leaves the world of young, free and single.'

Caspar was already looking over Helen's head towards the bar, and nodded to the wine waiter who was carrying trays of chilled champagne glasses with what looked like dry ice streaming out of them.

'I consider it my solemn duty to help my future bride achieve all her goals. Be right back with the drinks, ladies. Prepare to try the famous Kaplinski movie night cocktails.'

And with that he swaggered off across the polished floorboards with his shoulder pads leading the way.

Sara sighed and sat back in her chair. 'That man is almost good enough for you. Almost. And how is the birthday girl?'

Helen slapped her a little too vigorously on the back. 'Fan. Tastic. I need to catch up with the catering manager, and find out where your date has got to, but I will be right back. Stay put.'

'You are not going to leave me here on my own?' Sara could not hide the desperation in her voice.

'Of course not,' Helen replied, giving her one of her looks. 'Mingle, darling. Mingle. See you in five!'

Sara shook her head with a grin as Helen skipped her way through the crowd, then stopped to chat to a sword carrying pirate who had started a play fight with a young man waving a light sabre.

With a low chuckle, Sara lifted her evening bag higher onto her shoulder, sashayed out into the room and accepted a cool glass of cham-

pagne from a formally dressed waiter who
winked at her as he presented his silver tray.
She winked back. The young couple who ran
the village post office were always grateful for
extra work at the hotel and she could see his
wife on the other side of the room reorganising
the buffet display.

Fantastic! Now she had two more people to
chat to.

She was just about to turn away when a slim
man in a very stylish black suit, wearing white
gloves and a flowing cape with huge red lapels,
strolled into the room as though it was the deck
of a luxurious yacht. He held his body in a stiff
and mannered way—aloof and imposing. He
was dark and so classically handsome that Sara
could only gaze in awe. The gene fairy had certainly waved her magic wand over this boy.

All in all, he looked every inch the poster
boy for the modern city executive he no doubt
was. Polished and slick as steel. Confident in his
abilities and accustomed to taking charge in any
situation. A true captain of industry.

Sara gave a low sniff at the memory of all
the boys she had dated over the years who had
been clones of the man she was looking at. She
had been there, done that and had been disappointed time and again when it turned out that
they were far too interested in dating someone

who they could introduce to their family as the only daughter of Lady Fenchurch rather than find out who she was as a person.

Being at the end of a long line of aristocratic landowners certainly had its disadvantages. Especially when she did not have any rights to a title of her own.

Then Caspar instantly greeted him warmly and pointed him over towards the bar, except that as he turned away she caught a fleeting look on Count Dracula's face which she identified with only too well. It only lasted a fraction of a second but it spelt out that he felt lonely and foolish and out of place. Almost as though he had been dragged there and dressed up against his will.

Leo Grainger glanced around the room, then stared in horror as Caspar passed him a very odd-looking steaming drink. 'You do know that you are the one and only person on this planet who could drag me to Helen's birthday party dressed like this? I just thought you ought to know that. For the record.'

'What are friends for?' Caspar replied, waving his Kaplinski cocktail in the air. 'Think nothing of it. And no, I had nothing whatsoever to do with Helen setting you up with her old school friend. Sorry, pal, but she who must be

obeyed has decreed it so. Anyway, it is the least
I could do after you offered us the free use of
the hotel.'

Leo tipped his head and raised his glass towards Caspar's. 'It was my pleasure. There are
some compensations for being related to the
owner. I was happy to help. And Helen looks as
lovely as ever.'

'That she does,' Caspar replied, slapping Leo
on the back one handed and almost making him
spill his drink. 'Why don't you make a start on
the food? And while you're checking out the
buffet I'll check on my future bride. The lovely
Helen has some sort of surprise entertainment
up her sleeve to finish off the evening and I
want to be prepared. Back in a minute.'

And with that the gangster rolled across the
room, swaggering his shoulders dramatically
from side to side.

Leo blinked several times, shook his head,
took one sip of the cocktail, almost choked and
quickly picked up a glass of sparkling water
from a passing waiter with a smile and grateful
thanks. If that was the effect a Kaplinski cocktail had on an otherwise fairly normal lawyer
like Caspar, he would pass. For this job, he was
prepared to remain sober and very alert. And
risk the canapés.

Only as he peered across the room towards the

buffet table he was struck by something rather
remarkable. One of the elegant party guests was
talking to the waitress who was juggling empty
platters and plates. And not just idle chatting in
a condescending way but really laughing and
sharing a joke so that when she started jiggling
along and shaking her slim and very attractive
hips in time with the lively music playing in the
background, his own feet starting tapping with
them.

For the first time in days an ironic smile
creased the corner of Leo's mouth. He had so
many vivid memories about the rude and arro-
gant guests and diners he had served during his
days as a general waiter and dogsbody in his
aunt's hotel. They had been tough times when
he had been glad of the work but it had been
hard going and he had never truly got used to
being ignored or verbally abused—it had been
part of the training at the University of Life.

One thing he had learned was that a guest
who actually took the time to connect with the
serving staff and treat them as human beings
was a rare creature. The crowds cleared a little
and he could just make out that the tall brunette
with the short hair was even lovelier than he had
expected.

She was wearing a classic little black dress
and black evening gloves. Pearls, of course.

Elegant. Cool, but she still came over as somehow comfortable. That was it. She looked comfortable inside her own skin. She was not beautiful or sleek but somehow real with a natural prettiness and totally relaxed body language that she was not ashamed of.

The fact that her long slim legs tapered into lovely shapely ankles was an added bonus. This was no country bumpkin—this was an elegant and classy city girl who had been trapped here in the back of beyond like himself.

Perhaps he had found someone to talk to at this party after all.

CHAPTER TWO

SARA walked slowly along the buffet table, loading up her plate with bite-sized mouthfuls of the most delicious food. The hotel chef was amazing and, after three glasses of the Kaplinski cocktail whilst waiting for Helen, who was still mingling, she was in need of something more solid to add to her stomach. Her snatched lunchtime sandwich was a distant memory, and she wasn't entirely sure she had finished that. Okay, she was having a slight problem using the serving tongs while wearing long evening gloves which were slightly too large for her, but hunger had won out in the end and her reward was a plate heaped up with goodies.

The gloves were going to have to come off during the actual eating process—but some things were worth the sacrifice. And at this rate it would not take long for her to scoff the lot.

She had just paused at the mini pizza platter when the strains of a familiar musical theme song belted out above the background chatter. Her hand trembled as a tsunami of emotion and sentimental angst swept over her. All it took were a few lines of lyrics and the sound of a studio orchestra…and she unravelled.

It had always been the same. Sounds and music were associated for ever in her mind with specific people and places and events, and there was nothing she could do about it—that was the way her mind worked. All she had to do was hear the opening bars of a tune and she was right back in that moment.

Pity that it had to be now.

It had been a long busy week and the last thing she wanted was to walk into a party with a soundtrack playing music from one of her grandmother's favourite musicals. Just the memory of her grandmother holding her hand as they danced around this room, both singing at the top of their voices and having so much fun, was enough to get Sara feeling tearful.

She had so little left of her wonderful grandmother that even these memories seemed too precious to share in public.

No, she told herself sternly. She was not going to weep. This was Helen's birthday party! And she still had her grandmother's orchid houses—and they had meant more to her than anything else in this fine house. The fact that her grandmother had bequeathed them to her with the cottage was worth any amount of ridicule from her mother. She had trusted her to take care of them as their new custodian and that was precisely what she was doing.

So she had every reason to smile and pretend that everything was fine and she was just dandy! After everything Helen had done for her, she was not going to let her down. No way. Not going to happen. And so far her blind date had not appeared so she had this time to herself.

She needed a drink to ease the burning pain in her throat. That was all.

Sara quickly loaded up her plate with savoury bites, then paused in front of a superb dessert trolley. And right on top was a black satin-lined tray of chocolates which had been shaped into small award statuettes. Except that the few remaining chocolates had been crushed by other guests in their rush to gobble them up and from where she was standing looked more like body halves, with a luscious creamy-white centre. *Perfect.*

She had just scooped up some chocolate legs onto a silver spoon when there was a clatter and a loud beeping noise and Helen's distinctive voice called out from the centre of the room. Sara turned around just in time to see her friend stand on a chair holding a microphone in one hand and waving her basket in her other hand with such gusto that poor little stuffed Toto was joggling about and threatening to jump out at any minute.

'Hello, everyone. Me here. Thanks for coming. Just to let you know that there are five more minutes before the karaoke starts, so finish off your drinks and food and get ready to sing your heart out. Yes. That's right. Hollywood musicals. I just *know* it is going to be the best fun. Thanks.'

With that, Caspar strolled up and wrapped his arm around Helen's waist to lift her off the chair and back to the table, both of them laughing and so very happy. And, despite the fact that she wished her friends every joy, Sara felt her heart break as she watched Helen and Caspar clinging together. Was she ever going to find someone she wanted to be with who could return her love without seeing her as little more than an aristocratic trophy girl?

Sara was so distracted that it took her a second to realise that the other partygoers were making a sudden rush towards her and what was left on the buffet table. Drat. She would have to work fast to stock up before the hordes descended. Good thing she was at the dessert end of the queue. And with that she turned back to the trolley.

Only her way was blocked by the man in the

cape. And as she moved forward and he turned towards her, her hand banged into his arm and some of Sara's chocolate legs went flying onto the floor, narrowly missing his suit.

'Oh, I am so sorry,' she said, suddenly aware that she had not even realised that he was standing there as she reached across. 'How clumsy of me.'

Sara looked straight across into a pair of blue-grey eyes, the brightness backlit by the gentle light from a crystal chandelier over the buffet table. Their eyes locked for a moment, and something inside her flipped over. Several times.

This vampire was probably the best-looking man she had seen in a very long time. He had a long oval face with a strong chin and cheek-bones which could have been carved by a Renaissance sculptor, backed up by light Mediterranean colouring.

The only things that stopped her from melting into a pool at his feet were the deep frown lines between his heavy dark brown eyebrows. Perhaps he was as worried about the karaoke as she was?

Sara blinked several times. On the other hand, perhaps mixing allergy tablets with strange cocktails was not such a good idea and she should skip that question? But there was definitely something in the way he looked at her which had her skin standing to attention and her entire body waving *hello, handsome*!

'My fault entirely,' he replied 'Ah. Now it makes perfect sense. I came between a woman and her next chocolate fix. I now consider myself fortunate to have survived.'

He bent down and picked up what was left of the chocolate leg, which was now covered with a thick layer of whatever was on the fine parquet flooring from the feet of the guests. Only he squeezed it a little too hard, and the chocolate burst to release a gooey white chocolatey sticky mess over his white vampire costume gloves.

Sara held out a couple of napkins at arm's length. 'Don't get the chocolate on your gloves—you'll never get the stain out!'

Leo nodded wisely, tried to wipe the fragments of melted dark chocolate from the white fabric, gave up, then picked up a fresh piece of broken chocolate from the tray with his fingertips and bit into it. 'Might as well make the most of having messy fingers and be reckless. White fondant icing and bitter dark choc. Um…not too bad at all.'

Leo lifted the box from the display like a waiter and wafted them in front of Sara's nose.

'Miss Golightly, please allow me to replace your crushed confectionary in exchange for a nibble. And try saying that after one of Caspar's cocktails without getting slapped.'

Sara laughed out loud, making him raise his head, and he gave her a warm smile, which was slightly set off by the chocolate on his teeth—but warm nevertheless, with a certain twinkle in his eye which was infectious enough to make it impossible for her to refuse.

'Only if you can spare one, dear Count? How kind, thank you.'

Sara turned her head and nodded over her shoulder. 'All ready for your party piece? I have to warn you, Helen is relentless. Nobody will escape.'

He looked from side to side and leant closer, giving her a free whiff of a stunning body wash. 'Ze Prince of Darkness does not do diz party piece. No, no. It ees no elegant.'

'Can't sing for toffee?' Sara asked in a light voice, eyebrows raised.

His reply was a small shrug and a flip of one hand. 'So many talents.' Then he dropped his head and said through the corner of his mouth, 'Every dog in the village would start howling at the moon if I started singing. Tone deaf. Tried before. Crashed and burned. Not going to embarrass myself again.'

Sara was about to reply when a large gentleman in a huge gorilla suit joggled her arm en route to the buffet table, almost causing her to lose her dinner plate, and she had to snatch it away from catastrophe.

'I have a suggestion,' Sara whispered in her very best conspiratorial voice.

She glanced from side to side around the room. The way onto the patio was blocked by the karaoke machine and Helen and her work-mates, who were setting up some fiendish plan to persuade them all to sing. Drat! That was one exit down. *Time to get creative.*

'What would you say if I told you that I knew a secret exit onto the garden and we could escape the karaoke machine and eat our dinner in peace?'

Dracula's reply was to take a surprisingly firm hold around her waist, which made her gasp, and a firmer grip on his dinner plate before he whispered, 'I would tell you that I will follow you to the ends of the earth, my precious beauty. But make it fast. Caspar is on the prowl, looking for victims. And he has found a plastic machine gun.'

'Okay, now I am intrigued,' her fellow escapee whispered as they casually strolled along the wide terrace which ran around the full length of the hotel.

The sound of clinking glasses, tunes from the

classic musicals, really bad singing and lively chatter floated out into the summer evening through the open patio doors from the drawing room. Helen's party was in full swing but they had escaped and enjoyed their dinner in luxurious calm—and without the hindrance of evening gloves.

'How on earth did you know about that secret staircase leading down from the hall to the back door?'

Sara looked up at him and her lips curled into a smirk before she replied, 'Oh, I know every hidden passage and room and secret stair in that hotel. But of course you wouldn't know... I'm a local girl. In fact—' and at this she paused '—you might say I am *very* local.'

Then she took pity on his confusion, smiled and leant forward before adding, as casually as she could, 'I grew up in that house. Kingsmede Manor used to be my home.'

She stopped suddenly, dropped her shoulders back and pointed towards the upper floor of the building. 'Do you see the arched window with the stained glass? The room just at the corner on the left-hand side with the tiny balcony? That was my bedroom. I could lie in bed at night and watch the stars and the trees through the big picture window. It was magical!'

'Now I'm really confused,' he replied. 'Are

you telling me that your family used to own this house?'

'That's right,' she answered with a shrug. 'I am officially the last in the line of a family of Victorian eccentrics who built this house many generations ago. My grandmother passed away three years ago and left the whole place to my mother.'

Sara tilted her head and was grateful for the darkness in their corner of the garden so that he could not see the glint in her eyes. Talking about those sad times still hurt. 'Mum didn't want to live here—there were huge debts to clear and I'm sure you can imagine how expensive this house would be to run as a holiday home.' Sara waved one hand, then let it fall as she turned back to face him. 'And now it is this lovely hotel.'

'Wow,' he replied, with a look of something close to awe in his face. 'Are you serious? Did you really grow up in this amazing place?'

'Oh, yes,' she answered with a tiny shrug. 'I was sent to boarding school at the age of eight but this was the place I came back to every school holiday. We didn't have much money to spend on luxuries but it was paradise for a child.'

She stopped talking and stood still for a moment, her eyes scanning the whole front of the building. 'I have wonderful memories of my life here.' She turned back to him with a smile and raised her eyebrows to ask with a lift in her voice, 'How about you? What is your old castle like back in Transylvania?'

'Oh, the usual problems of living in a dungeon,' he replied with a sniff. 'You just cannot get the staff these days. Draughty. Cold. There is a lot to be said for central heating.'

'Oh, I so agree,' Sara said with a nod. 'The modern vampire needs his central heating.'

'Even so,' Dracula said, leaning against a wrought-iron balustrade at the edge of the terrace and peering out across the grounds in front of the house, 'I envy you growing up here.'

Sara moved closer so that she could stand next to him with her arms stretched out on the metal railing. The cherry trees in front of the house had been strung with white party lights so the front entrance looked like a picture from a children's fairy tale. A pergola filled with climbing white roses and multicoloured clematis in pinks and purples had been built on the western side of the house to capture the last rays of the setting sun and as Sara and the vampire looked out onto the lawns a light breeze lifted the perfume and surrounded them with warmth and fragrance.

It was a magical evening and Sara felt her

shoulders relax for the first time in many days.
A new moon appeared in the night sky, which
was clear and already twinkling with the first
stars.

She was suddenly very glad that she had accepted Helen's invitation to the party.

This was why she'd never found peace when
she'd lived in London. It had never come close
to this special place in her life.

She leant in contented silence and grasped
the balustrade with both hands and inhaled the
warm air and the warm atmosphere drifting out
from the party, which was going on quite well
without them. She was also aware of how very
close she was standing next to this man she had
only just met. Close enough that she could hear
his breathing and the way his cloak rustled in
the slight breeze, silk on silk.

This was new! It had been a long time since
she had spent the evening alone with a handsome man. Especially one content to enjoy the
view in silence. He seemed happy to allow her
to do all the talking but she was relaxed enough
in his presence to chatter on about nothing in
particular.

Of course he knew very little about her and
they could enjoy the type of conversation that
could only happen between strangers, unfet-
tered by past history.

Perhaps she should start talking about orchids and fertiliser and the poor man would run away for help? As it was, she knew Helen would soon send out a search party to track her down so that she could be introduced to her blind date whether she liked it or not.

A twinge of guilt made Sara wince. Caspar's friend was probably inside, feeling most neglected and rejected. She should go in and face the music in more ways than one.

Soon.

She would go in soon.

She could stand here for another few minutes and enjoy herself before going back to the party and throwing herself into Helen's celebrations. She was not going to spend her best friend's party hiding in the garden feeling sorry for herself or mourning the life she had once known. Especially when she had such a good listener as a companion.

'I don't come here very often,' she whispered, even though there was only the two of them on the terrace. 'My cottage is just across the lane so I can see the house every day if I want. But this garden is for hotel guests now, not previous residents. This is a rare treat.'

'That's because you love this place so much and you miss it,' he replied in a gentle voice and chuckled at her gasp of surprise. 'Yes. It is fairly obvious. Especially…'

'Especially?' Sara asked in a shaky breath. She was not used to opening up to a complete stranger in this way and it startled her, and yet was strangely reassuring. *Weird.*

'I was going to say, especially considering that your family sent you away to boarding school when you were only eight years old.' He blew out hard and blinked. 'Eight! That's hard for me to get my head around. You must have been so miserable.'

Miserable? How did she even begin to explain to a stranger the misery of leaving her home in the middle of the most traumatic time of her life? Abandoned by her mother, who didn't know what to do with her. Worse, by the father she adored, who thought he was doing the right thing by leaving them to start a new life in South America when the life of luxury he'd thought he had married into when he'd chosen a girl with an aristocratic title and a country estate had completely failed to materialise.

Her whole world had shifted under her feet and was still shifting now. Even after three years of living in her tiny cottage, there were some days when she had to remind herself that she had a home that no one could take away from her. She might be unloved but she would never again be homeless and rootless. She had sold everything she had and burnt her bridges to make the orchid nursery a reality—but it was hers.

Sara blinked hard. The blur of constant activity which she used to fill each day created a very effective distraction, but even talking about those sad times brought memories percolating up into her consciousness. Memories she had to put back in their place where they belonged.

Selling the house and most of the contents had been the price her mother had to pay for the chance for them both to be independent. But it had still been incredibly painful.

Instinctively, she felt the man in the black costume looking at her, watching her, one elbow on the metal railing, waiting for her to give him an answer to this question.

She turned slightly towards him and noticed for the first time, in the light from the party room and the twinkling stars in the trees, that his eyes were not grey but a shade of blue like the ocean at dusk. And at that moment those eyes were staring very intently at her.

On another day and another time she might even have said that he was more gorgeous than merely handsome. He was certainly striking and wore the cape and costume as though it had been made for him.

Allure of this quality did not come cheap.

It was a shame that she had sworn off dating for at least a year or two until she had a new greenhouse up and running. Until then, she could keep her loneliness to herself and wear her happy face to the world, even if it was a struggle sometimes.

'Oh,' she said, 'they had their reasons. And it wasn't all bad. I knew that I would always have this home to come back to in the holidays. My grandmother had such fun here. She loved this old house, especially the gardens.'

'The gardens?' he asked and his hand swept out towards the long stretches of simple grass lawns. 'What was so special about the gardens? They seem pretty normal to me.'

'Oh,' she breathed, and a great grin creased her face. 'The gardens then were nothing like they are today. They were…extraordinary. Unique. People used to come for miles just to see the gardens of this house.' Sara turned back to face the lawns and gestured past the cherry trees towards the beech hedges and the long drive to the lane. 'It's only a few minutes' walk to Kingsmede village from here and the gardens were somehow part of the community. She used to hold the most remarkable parties here. The local village fete, of course. Then there were weddings, birthday parties and all kinds of local and family events.'

She flicked a smile at Dracula, who was still watching her, almost as though he was studying her. 'I can remember my grandmother's eightieth birthday party as though it was yesterday. We started in the afternoon with most of the village turning up for afternoon tea, and then moved on to dinner with a live band with dancing and singing. Then there were fireworks. Lots of fireworks.'

Sara shook her head but when she spoke her voice trailed away. 'It was a magical night. The end of an era, I suppose.' Then she looked up into the sky at the new moon and felt the sting of tears in the corners of her eyes as the memory of the event swirled through her. She was so captivated by the intense memory of her grandmother dancing in her ballgown and jewels, and the music and the fairy lights and trees, that when Dracula shifted next to her on the railing, she suddenly came crashing down to earth with the harsh reality that those moments and those parties were long gone like the gardens that used to be here.

'Oh, I'm so sorry,' she said through a tight, sore throat. 'Here I am, rambling on about people you don't know and a world which has already long gone. How embarrassing! I don't usually go on about the house like this. The hotel company own it now and there's nothing I can do about that. But thank you for listening.'

Dracula inclined his head towards her. 'I got the feeling that you needed to talk. Apparently I was right. And you weren't boring, not in the least.'

He took a step closer in the fading light and in the harsh shadows his cheekbones were sharp angles and his chin strong and resolute. His body was tall and slim but anything but boyish.

Just the opposite. The masculine strength and power positively beamed out from every pore and grabbed her. It was in the way he held his body, the way his head inclined just that tiny fraction of an inch as he looked at her as though she was the most fascinating woman he had ever met, and oh, yes, the laser focus of those intelligent blue-grey eyes had a lot to do with it as well.

He was so close that she could touch him if she wanted to. In the calm tranquillity of their pergola she could practically feel the softness of his breath on her skin as he gazed intently into her eyes. Loud laughter and bright music was playing somewhere in the house but all of her senses were totally focused on this man who had outspokenly captivated her.

She couldn't move.

She did not want to move.

And then he did something extraordinary. He leant forward so that their bodies were almost touching and she sucked in a breath, terrified, exhilarated and excited. Was he going to kiss her? But, with a faint smile, he lifted his chin, his eyes broke away from hers and he reached out to the climbing rose behind her head and stepped back a second later with a perfect full white rose.

She stared, wide-eyed, as he swept his thumb and forefinger down the stem with his naked hand.

'A lovely rose for a lovely lady. No thorns allowed. May I?'

Completely at a loss as to what he was asking permission to do, Sara simply nodded and smiled as he stretched out his hand, lifted her left wrist towards him and carefully pressed the rose stem under the jewelled strap of her watch.

'I never had more than a window box growing up, so I am totally clueless when it comes to flowers,' he murmured in a smooth warm voice. 'But I hope you will accept this small token as a pitiful excuse for a wrist corsage.'

She smiled and bit her lower lip, and was instantly grateful for the cover of darkness to cover up her blushes. 'It's lovely. Thank you.'

'Excellent,' he replied and stepped back and

extended both arms, his cloak flapping behind him. 'Well, that only leaves one more special request to complete the evening.' He twirled his right hand in the air and gave a dramatic short bow from the waist. 'May I have the pleasure of this dance, young lady? I shall try not to step on your toes or spread chocolate on the back of your dress.'

'Well,' Sara replied with a sigh and looked from side to side on the deserted terrace, 'my dance card is already quite full, but I suppose I could spare you a few minutes.'

Instantly she found his right hand resting lightly at her waist, and her right hand resting lightly inside his fingers. 'They're playing our song.' He smiled and drew her closer towards him so that the front of his black jacket was just touching her chest.

Stunned by being pressed against him by a firm hand in the small of her back, Sara blinked hard, swallowed down a gulp of shock and paid attention. 'We have a song?' she asked, then looked up from his shoes to find him smiling deep into her eyes.

'Of course.' He grinned and stepped forward with his right foot, then shifted onto his left, carrying her with him onto the wider part of the terrace. 'Just listen,' he whispered into her ear, and moved gracefully from side to side.

It was a waltz. A dreamy concoction from a long gone world of Viennese dancing in crystal ballrooms, captured for ever on celluloid and movie soundtrack albums so that she could listen to those soaring strings in a country garden in England, through the open patio doors of a party. And it took her breath away.

Sara was so entranced that it took her a second to realise that her feet were moving instinctively into the waltz positions she had been taught at school all those years ago.

'I know what you're thinking,' her dance partner whispered and she opened her eyes to find him smiling down at her. 'Is the Danube really blue? And are there woods in Vienna?'

'Ah. Caught me out,' she tutted back, suddenly grateful that he did not know what she had actually been thinking, which had a lot more to do with just how close their bodies were pressed together.

'I do have one question,' he said in a low voice. 'Don't you find it difficult to go back into the house as just a normal guest?'

'Yes, I do,' she answered as truthfully as she could. 'But I couldn't miss the chance to catch up with Helen for a few hours. We lead such busy lives these days.'

And then Sara tilted her head and looked up at the tall man whose eyes had rarely left hers for the whole time that they had been out on the terrace.

'And how about you? How do you know Caspar? I noticed you chatting when you came in and, no offence, but you don't look like a lawyer.'

The corner of his mouth turned up into a small smile which even in this light seemed to illuminate his face and soften the harsh contours, making it even more handsome than it was before.

'None taken,' he replied and pursed his lips. 'Caspar used to date my younger sister. And I think it's time for a twirl.' He stepped back as the music soared to a crescendo and lifted his left arm high above her head, just far enough so that Sara could turn around in probably the worst twirl under the sun, but they were both laughing at the end of it.

Judging by the applause and cheers that burst forth from the party, they had not been the only ones who had tried to match the music with some dancing.

Instantly the music shifted to a loud song from a children's cartoon sung by dancing kitchen utensils and her vampire looked at her and shrugged.

'I agree,' Sara murmured and shook her head. 'I think that's my signal to sit the next dance out. But thank you, kind sir. And now it is my turn for a question. Isn't that a little awkward?' she asked as his hands released her and she felt in desperate need of a distraction to fill the growing space between them. 'Seeing Caspar with Helen? You do know that they adore each other?'

He raised an eyebrow and chuckled as he leant back against the railing. 'I certainly hope so since I have been invited to their wedding. But no, it isn't a problem. In fact I'm pleased for him. It was years ago, my sister is happily married and quite pregnant and Caspar has found someone who loves him. Good luck to them both.'

Then he turned sideways. 'You dance beautifully. And in fact I should be thanking you for helping me to make a lucky escape.'

He chuckled loudly and thrust both hands deep into the trouser pockets of his tuxedo trousers. 'The lovely Helen had set me up on a blind date! Can you believe it? I am sure her old school friend is absolutely charming but there is no way that I intend to date a country girl who needs Helen's help to find an escort for the evening. Thank you but no. I don't do country. Never have, never will.'

Sara very slowly and carefully moved closer to the handrail so that she could gaze out over the lawns without looking at the vampire. Was it possible? Was this the famous Leo that Helen was trying to set her up with? Caspar's friend?

She almost groaned out loud. Of course! Who else would it be?

Sara's cheeks burned with humiliation and embarrassment. How could she have been so stupid? She was never going to live this one down.

Now what did she do? Tell the truth? Try and laugh it off and save them both the embarrassment? What were the alternatives? After all, she already knew that he would be an usher at Helen and Caspar's wedding, so there was no escaping him. But right now at this minute he had no idea that she was the country bumpkin in question.

She glanced up at him and instant regret fluttered through her.

Just when she was enjoying this man's company, there was a sting in the tail. He was handsome, generous and a good listener. Those were good credentials for any date. Helen certainly did good work except for one tiny thing. This man had no intention of going out on a blind date with her, just as she had no intention of going out with him.

Suddenly all the enjoyment of her waltz in the moonlight seemed to drift away into the air like smoke in the wind. Every spark of energy and enthusiasm was extinguished, leaving behind a sad and pathetic girl whose friends took pity on her.

Dracula was right. She had become the country girl he so clearly despised, just as her mother had predicted she would. Clumsy, gauche, uncultured and unattractive. Destined for a life alone because no decent man would look twice at her. She could just hear her mother's voice, drenched with disgust and disappointment, on the day after the funeral when her ex-boyfriend had dumped her and taken off back to London as fast as his sports car could take him.

Well, it looks like you were right, Mum.

Suddenly the enormity of everything that was happening in her life seemed to crash down on her, and Sara shivered in her sleeveless shift dress. There was no way that she could go back into the party now.

It was time to go home. And back to the insular life she had created for herself and all of the harsh realities that lay there—and definitely without this man who had treated her as an equal for an hour. He looked so handsome and clearly successful, while she was a walking advert for a mess.

'Feeling cold?' Dracula asked and, without waiting for a reply, he reached behind his shoulders and slipped off the scarlet-lined cape and

draped it in a single swirl of his wrists around
her neck so that it fell almost to her bracelets in
a cocoon of body-warmed fabric. Sara inhaled
the perfume of the man's body and, despite her
best efforts to resist, pulled the fabric closer
around her so that his warmth penetrated her
goose-fleshed arms and the shivering died away.

'Thank you,' she murmured but still could
not look him in the eye. 'If you'll excuse me, I
think I'll head home for the evening. It has been
a long busy week. I'll make sure that Caspar
returns the cape to you before you leave. Thank
you for your company.'

'Hey, wait a moment, Cinderella,' he replied
as she lifted her head and tried to walk casually
back to the side gate which led to her cottage.
'Did you say that you were staying across the
lane? Please allow me to see you home. It is the
very least I can do, seeing as you gave me such
a lucky escape.'

And, before she could accept or decline,
Dracula stepped in place beside her and they
strolled side by side across the lawns and away
from the house in silence. Her throat burning
with humiliation, her eyes stinging. Incapable
of speech.

CHAPTER THREE

SOMEWHERE in her bedroom a full symphony orchestra was playing what should have been a soothing overture to a lovely ballet. Except, to Sara's ears, the instruments sounded as though they had been tuned in a sawmill.

She stirred and tugged the duvet farther towards her chin, then yawned loudly. The first thing on her to-do list that morning would be to retune the radio to a popular music channel.

She tried to snuggle back to sleep, but there was something uncomfortable on her pillow.

She reached up until her fingers closed around a string of pearls.

Oh, no! She must have slept in them all night. There would probably be bobble-shaped marks all over her neck and chin.

Never mind. It was early. She still had plenty of time to recover from last night and get smartened up before her meeting at the hotel.

Last night! Ah, the party. That would explain

why she felt so weary. She ran her tongue over her parched lips. Juice. She needed juice. Then tea would be good.

Her eyes flickered slowly open and both hands lifted the duvet as she glanced down.

Helen Lewis had a lot to answer for. It had been years since she had been so tired that she had crawled into bed in her underwear. Sara glanced around her bedroom and, sure enough, her black dress lay across the armchair at the foot of her bed.

Sara was still mentally shaking her head when an Abyssinian ball of fur and mischief launched itself onto the duvet and sashayed up, until Sara could scratch between his ears.

'Oh, Pasha, you know that you are not allowed in here.'

She laughed as the rich golden brown cat purred with pleasure, then started nudging her face, the cute red nose pushing against her neck so he could play with the pearls that she was still wearing.

'Ready for breakfast? Good. I'll head for the shower and repair the damage before anyone sees me.'

Sara pushed back the covers and swung her legs over the edge of the bed. It took a second or two before her world stopped spinning, but at least she was on her feet and ready to get to work. She had a lot to do today and not much time to do it in.

She was still feeling dreamy and slightly dazed when her toes crushed down onto something round and hard on the soft handmade rug that had come with the cottage when she inherited it...

She dared not look down.

Oh, please, not something else her cat had brought in.

Sure enough, Pasha came sidling up to her and started rubbing himself up and down her legs.

'Pasha, if you have been in the kitchen bin again, you are in so much trouble!'

Her grandmother's old cat had a knack for finding something from the floor to play with. Loose screws, plant ties, paperclips—they all ended up being scooped out and played with. And Helen had brought bags of treasures with her when they played dress up before the party.

Sara knew from personal experience that all jewellery and shiny small items had to be locked securely away unless she wanted them to be redistributed around the cottage as cat toys.

'Okay. Let's find out what you've brought me this time!'

Sara moved her foot and glanced down at the floor.

And stopped breathing.

It was a button. A large black button with a silver scroll on it. The sort of button that might be used on a coat. Or a black evening cloak. The kind of cloak a vampire count might wrap around a girl's shoulders late in the evening. For example.

Eloise Sara Jane Marchant Fenchurch de Lambert had many doubts in life, but one thing was certain.

That button had not come from any garment she owned.

Suddenly she felt dizzy and collapsed back on her bed, trying to ignore Pasha, who was headbutting her legs.

Breathe deeply. That was the secret. Inhale, and then exhale slowly. Slowly.

She clasped both hands to the top of her head.

Think. Think. Last night. What was the last thing she could remember from last night? Her eyes clenched shut.

The party. Dracula. Sharing her buffet dinner…with Dracula. Escaping onto the terrace and walking around the garden and talking and dancing…with Dracula. Then Dracula turned into Caspar's friend Leo instead of a bat and offered to walk her home. Then? Nothing specific. Her cottage. He opened the front door for her. Lights.

Her eyes opened just in time to see Pasha playing with the button between his paws.

Of course! She had been wearing his heavy cloak on their short walk from the hotel, but she had slipped it off as soon as she was inside and handed it back. The button must have come loose and Pasha had brought it in.

A great whoosh of relief came out of Sara's mouth and her shoulders dropped six inches.

Sara reached forward and snatched the button away from her cat before it was completely clawed to pieces.

'Sorry, Pasha. I need to give this back to Caspar so he can return it to his vampire friend.'

Shaking her head, Sara pushed herself off the bed and across the corridor to her plain white-tiled bathroom. This was going to be a two coffee morning if she had any chance at all of impressing the Events Manager at the hotel. It had not been easy to arrange a meeting on a weekend, but this was her one chance to convince him that Kingsmede Manor should choose Cottage Orchids for all their flower displays.

Of course she had made light of her business plans in front of Helen—her friend was getting married in a few weeks and she didn't want to worry her with finances, but a regular contract with the hotel would make a difference to her investment plans. She had so many exciting ideas for the next twelve months! It would be wonderful if she could transform at least some of them into reality.

No pressure then. Oh, no.

The Venetian glass mirror with its silver surround had been her grandmother's—and one of the few precious things her mother had allowed her to bring from the old house, only because the hotel did not want it. There was a chip in the frame where the mirror had once fallen off the wall when the plaster had got too wet to take the weight, but Sara didn't mind.

She brushed her hair out and peered at the glass. Not too bad considering she had slept in her make-up. The red lipstick was gone, probably onto the pillowcase. Time to hit the shower; she needed to be sharp this morning and it was already… Oh, what time was it?

And then Sara made the mistake of looking for her wristwatch. Which she had left on the basin the evening before. Same as always.

Only it wasn't there.

Her watch had been lifted away from the basin and any potential splashes onto a higher shelf. And in its place next to the soap dish was a solid white metal ring with a solitaire diamond in the centre.

Her fingers were shaking as she reached out

and lifted the ring onto her finger. It was huge, just fitting her thumb. It was a man's ring.

She slowly turned around and looked left, half dreading what she might see.

The dressing gown she had left on the side of the bath the night before when she was rushing to get changed for the party was hanging up behind the bathroom door. And her fluffy hand towel was hanging from the towel rail so that the lavender embroidered design on the bottom was straight and parallel to the floor.

This was very nice, except that when she used the hand towel it usually ended up being tossed over the side of the bath or the basin. In fact, it was a standing joke that if you wanted to find a towel in Sara's house you had to look anywhere but on the towel rail.

Someone had hung up her dressing gown and used her hand towel. And that someone was not Helen, who was so used to Sara's quirky habits that she had long since given up clearing up in her wake.

The only thing that had not been moved in her bathroom was the indoor drying rack across the top of the bath. Her smartest lace bras and panties were still stretched out to dry, complete with frayed edges, re-sewn straps and labels which had been washed so many times that the print had worn away.

And then she saw what had been staring her in the face the whole time.

Her toilet seat was up and standing to attention.

Two seconds later, the scream that came from Sara's mouth drove Pasha through the bathroom and under the bed.

'Leo, you idiot! When was the last time you saw it?'

Leo Grainger groaned and pinched the bridge of his nose between his thumb and forefinger. There were very few people in this world who knew him well enough to call him an idiot to his face, but Caspar was one of them, and this time he could well be right.

'I know I was wearing it before I put the white gloves on to go out to the party, and then in the hotel bathroom when I took it off to wash my hands. After that. No clue.'

'The bathroom?' Caspar shrugged and stared at his friend in amazement. 'Who takes their ring off when they wash their hands?'

'I do. Always have. You know that ring is one of the few things I have left from my dad, so I take care of it. Okay?'

'Okay, okay.' Caspar raised both hands in submission and helped himself to more toast. 'What about after the party? I noticed you escaped the karaoke by taking off with Sara Fenchurch. Any chance you lost it in the gardens…? What? What did I say?'

Leo dropped his head to the table and knocked it twice on the breakfast tablecloth before groaning and sitting back with his eyes closed, grateful for the fact that Caspar had come to Leo's hotel room for room service breakfast.

'Sara? As in blind date Sara? That was the girl in the black dress and gloves?'

Caspar waved his buttered toast in Leo's direction. 'Sure. I saw you chatting at the buffet and the next thing I knew you were out on the terrace and…' The truth slowly dawned on Caspar and he sighed out loud. 'You did know that the girl you were feeding chocolates to was…'

Leo shook his head from side to side and closed his eyes.

'Ah. Right. So Helen hadn't introduced you after all.'

And then Caspar cheered up and leant across and thumped Leo on the arm.

'Does my lady love do good work or does she not? I told you that Sara was a great girl! Helen will be ecstatic. She adores Sara and apparently the girl went through a rough time before we met but, hey, good on you both. What? What?'

Leo stared cold-eyed across the table at

Caspar. 'Do you think that Sara knew who I was? Before the party?'

'Of course,' Caspar replied, rolling his eyes and reaching for the marmalade. 'Helen always gives her friends a full colour dossier on any bloke she wants them to hook up with.'

'So Sara didn't know who I was before we met?'

Caspar shrugged. 'She would probably never have spoken to you if she had. I got the impression Sara was just as impressed with the idea of being set up on a blind date as you were. Why? Does that make a difference?'

'It might. It's amazing what a Kaplinski cocktail and a heavy dose of moonlight and nostalgia can do. She got upset and I ended up walking her back to her place across the lane.'

There was silence for a few seconds, before Caspar lowered his voice to reply. 'Walked her home…?'

Leo nodded once.

Caspar glanced towards the door before going on. 'Anything I should know before Helen arrives? Because these girls tell each other everything. And I mean everything.' He blinked several times.

'I escorted her to the door, saw her inside, then went to the bathroom before I left,' he replied in a low voice. 'She was already asleep by the time I came out.'

Caspar sighed in relief and rubbed his hands together. 'That's better. Now we're getting somewhere. All you have to do is call Sara and ask if she found a man's ring in her bathroom this morning. Simple. Right? Leo? Why are you shaking your head at me like that? You know who she is and where she lives.'

Leo made eye contact with Caspar and squeezed his eyes together. Tight. And winced. 'Oh, yes. Right after I tell her that I slipped her dress off and tucked her in last night. That is going to go down well, especially when I have to stand next to her and smile at your wedding at some point in the near future.'

'You undressed her?' There was amazement in Caspar's voice, even a touch of awe and horror. 'Oh, that is so not good. Did you know that Helen and Sara used to call themselves the two Musketeers at school? Upset one, upset both of them.'

'Thanks! I'm looking for some useful advice here. I need my father's ring back before I meet up with my aunt and the rest of the clan on Friday, and you need to keep the lovely Helen from drowning me in the fountain outside.'

'I'm thinking, I'm thinking.' Caspar started drumming his fingers on the table. 'We need

to come up with something so wonderful that
Sara and Helen will forget any embarrassment
and love you for ever.' Then his fingers stilled
on a small crystal vase containing three cut pink
orchid blossoms. 'Of course. Flowers. Helen is
worried about the state of Sara's business.'

Caspar leant over the table and grinned. 'Leo,
my friend? How would you like to become the
lovely Sara's knight in shining armour and get
your father's ring back at the same time? Time
to put some of those Rizzi family connections
to good use, my man.'

Sara Fenchurch pretended to look for something
in her briefcase until everyone else had left the
hotel reception area before gingerly stepping out
and walking calmly to the Events Manager's
office, smiling as she went and hoping nobody
could see her shaking.

She was two minutes early for her appoint-
ment. Two minutes to somehow calm her racing
pulse and steady her nerves just long enough to
convince the Events Manager, Mr Evans, that
he should choose her plant nursery for all of his
weddings and special occasions. This could be
a terrific new order.

If only she could get past her nerves about
asking for work. She always hated this part
of running her business. Helen said it was the

whole idea that she was relying on another person to decide whether to choose her nursery, or not. And she was spot on.

Sara had already spent far too many years doing what other people expected her to do, how they wanted her to do it and generally performing like a trained seal in a circus. Doing whatever she had to for their approval.

Until three years ago, she had lived her life according to other people's rules. That life had ended on the day she had started making decisions on her own. Good or bad. Safe or reckless. She was responsible for making her own way in the world now.

The orchid business had given her back some of the self-confidence she had lost, then had added more than she'd ever had before. It had taken most of her savings but it was working, and she was making enough to live on. Now she was ready to move up and on and take her passion to the next level.

This was her business and she was a businesswoman and she needed customers like this hotel.

Head up, shoulders back. *She was going in.*

Except that just as she stretched out her hand to knock, the fine panelled door was flung open and she almost rapped her knuckles on the nose of the man she had come to see.

'Well, good morning to you, Miss Fenchurch. And right on time,' he gushed and shook her hand with so much enthusiasm that his trendy wraparound spectacles joggled on the end of his nose. 'Tony Evans. Delighted to see you again so soon. I do so admire punctuality. May I offer you some tea or coffee? And do come in. I would like to get started as soon as possible.'

She managed a smile by biting the inside of her mouth to conceal her astonishment at the warm welcome. 'Thank you, Mr Evans, but I'm fine, thanks.'

By some miracle, her legs still worked as she followed the Events Manager into the palatial office which had once been the butler's room and sat neatly down, stiff backed and silent, until he had collapsed his substantial girth into the huge leather chair on the other side of the desk.

'You know what makes this hotel special, Sara?' he asked, pointing out of the window across the beautiful gardens. 'And I hope you don't mind me calling you Sara, but I just know that we are going to get on famously.'

He did not wait for a reply before going on. 'The small details. Our guests want something special and luxurious and that is what we aim to give them. And they want our suppliers to be local. Low carbon footprint and all of that. And we can't get much more local than your plant nursery, can we?'

Before she could answer, Tony Evans whipped his chair around and clasped his neatly manicured hands in front of her.

'I want you to be one of those suppliers, Sara. I've been looking at that portfolio of arrangements you sent me and I like what I've seen. I know quality when I see it. You've got potential, young lady. And I'm willing to take a risk on you.'

Sara sucked in a discreet breath. *This was it.* After three years of working seven days a week, someone was going to take a chance on her, based on the plants she had grown with her own hands. And, best of all—*most precious of all*—she had done this on her own.

Nobody had pulled strings to get her into a job or a step ahead in the line by using her aristocratic connections.

This was all her own work, and her heart leapt so fast she almost cried.

'A risk, Mr Evans?' her voice squeaked in reply.

'This hotel has events scheduled for every weekend until Valentine's Day next year. Right now, we have two florists working on cut flower arrangements for every room in the hotel as well as special events. I need you to prove to me that

I can cut the carbon footprint and provide consistent high quality within budget by choosing you to do the same job.'

He passed a blue folder across the desk to Sara, who could only stare at it, stunned, as he stabbed his forefinger onto the cover several times.

'Inside this wallet are the plans for the biggest corporate weekend of the year. I want to see how you would handle an event this size before I sign any contracts.'

Sara glanced at the first page of the dossier and breathed out very, very, slowly. 'This is a big project but I will try to work through some proposals and get back to you in a few weeks. If that is okay...Mr Evans?'

He paused, then startled her by leaning back in his chair and crossing his arms.

'Our client is on a tight schedule. He has already asked for a detailed cost breakdown and I promised that it would be with him by next Friday at the latest.'

Sara sat in silence for a few seconds before replying in a squeak. 'That's wonderful and so exciting, but do you really mean *next* Friday? As in five days from now?'

Tony Evans nodded in silence, arms still crossed.

Sara swallowed hard before replying. 'I appreciate your vote of confidence, but I really would like more time to…'

'Our current florists are very keen to continue supplying this hotel,' he interrupted, 'and indeed all of the other hotels in the group, so it would be terrific if you could show us the benefits of choosing a local supplier instead of a large company. Don't you agree?'

Sara blinked and tried not to jump onto her chair and punch her fist in the air. Other hotels? Oh, yes. She could supply the other hotels in the group. No trouble at all.

'Of course I have every confidence that you will come up with something spectacular. Leo Grainger tells me that you are the best in the business and I couldn't have a better recommendation than that.'

Sara's eyes flicked open and she stared at Tony Evans in disbelief.

'Leo?' she asked incredulously and cleared her throat. 'Leo Grainger recommended my orchids?'

'He did indeed,' Tony replied and tapped the side of his nose, 'and in glowing terms. That is quite something from a man with his reputation.' And then he paused and frowned at her. 'I confess I was a little concerned about how you are going to manage with your relocation. Finding land to rent around the village is not going to be easy. But I am sure you will let us know your new contact details.'

In an instant all thoughts of Leo Grainger were swept away and Sara sprang back into full focus. 'Relocation?' she replied with a broken smile. 'I'm sorry but there must be some mis-understanding. I have no plans to relocate.'

The smile dropped from Tony's face and he pushed his chin out. 'Ah. You should have received the letter from our managing agents saying that the lands you rent from us will no longer be available from later this year. Part of our redevelopment plan. Big part.'

The air crackled as Sara tried to pull herself together long enough to ask what on earth he was talking about, when the telephone started ringing. 'I'm so sorry but I shall have to take this,' he said with obvious relief in his voice. 'Shall I expect to see your proposals for the event in time for me to agree to them before Friday, Sara? Excellent. Have a great day.'

Sara was just about to turn away, when she looked back over one shoulder and casually asked, 'Leo Grainger. How exactly do you know him?'

'Oh, apparently Leo is related to the owners. Works as some sort of business consultant,' Tony Evans replied with a shrug, his hand over the telephone mouthpiece. 'Okay, Sara? Friday?'

Seconds later, Sara stood in the corridor feeling as though the cream-and-gold carpet has been whipped out from under her feet.

Leo Grainger was a business consultant who had been in her bedroom, seen her underwear and straightened her towels.

Worse. He was related to the famous Rizzi family of hoteliers who had bought the Manor.

No wonder he had actually thanked her for saving him from a terrible blind date—her!

But then he had recommended her business to the hotel team.

What was going on? Did he feel sorry for her?

With a groan, her fingers tightened around the handle of her briefcase and she remembered the file Tony Evans had just given her.

Suddenly she didn't know whether to kiss Leo in grovelling thanks for opening the door to this amazing opportunity, or kick him hard in the shins for making her feel so worthless and pathetic as a woman.

She closed her eyes and took a breath.

She *should* be grateful that Leo had recommended her work to the hotel—it was a nice thing for him to do.

Except somehow she felt deflated and disappointed.

This was totally crazy! She *should* be enthusiastic. It was just that for a precious few seconds she had thought that she had earned this opportunity because of her own hard work. Instead of which, the decision had been influenced by connections to the powerful people who demanded respect and got it.

But what choice did she have? This was a terrific opportunity which she was going to seize with both hands.

Sara sighed and started to walk towards the curving staircase that led to the guest bedrooms. Helen and Caspar would be heading back to London soon for Sunday lunch with Caspar's parents. This was the ideal time to give Helen Leo's ring, which she had found in her bathroom, and try to laugh off her embarrassment about the blind date.

Or perhaps the famous Leo was feeling a little guilty about his parting comments? Helen and Caspar would have already grilled him over breakfast about how the blind date had gone. If he didn't know who she was last evening, he certainly would know by now.

And she had his ring.

Then Sara stopped at the foot of the staircase and thought for a second.

No. If Leo Grainger the famous business consultant wanted his ring back, he was going to have to come and ask her for it. That way, she could thank him in person for his recommendation and clear the air, for Helen's sake as well as her own.

It would be humiliating, but she could face him and get the embarrassment over and done with. Whatever Leo's reasons for helping her.

In the meantime, she had to call the letting agent. And fast. She didn't want any more of her clients being worried with silly rumours about her moving the orchid nursery. What a ridiculous idea!

That land had been the old kitchen gardens of this house and her grandmother had only sold it to pay for the roof repairs on condition that she could keep her orchid houses in a tiny corner next to the gardener's cottage.

There was no way that the farmer would sell the land to the hotel. Was there?

CHAPTER FOUR

LEO GRAINGER raised his right hand and waved as Caspar and Helen drove slowly away from the hotel and back to their happy London life, leaving him standing in the car park feeling rather like a teenager left at boarding school watching his parents drive away, while he was left alone in a land where he didn't totally understand the local rules and customs.

The feeling was so ridiculous that he shrugged away a moment of disquiet inside his black cashmere jacket before lifting his chin and strolling out onto the stone terrace.

His aunt Arabella had seen something unique and special about Kingsmede Manor, and he certainly trusted her judgement. She had impeccable taste with a superb eye for detail and for spotting the potential of a property, a skill she had built up over a lifetime spent in the hotel trade at every level around the world.

His footsteps slowed and he paused for a

minute to admire the imposing stone house in the bright sunlight on a Sunday morning in rural England. Yesterday evening the hotel had been in shadow from the twinkly bulbs scattered amongst the trees and the electric light streaming out from the windows, but this morning it seemed to have more of its own personality.

His mother had grown up in a house like this in Italy—he had seen photographs of the palazzo his grandfather had built after years of creating one of the most successful hotel chains in Europe.

It was magnificent in every respect. Opulent and imposing. The whole building designed with the express purpose to impress and impose a vision of the owner and the power and wealth required to build it, without a hint of the sacrifices the family had made to achieve that wealth.

The rest of the world considered his grandfather to be a successful and brilliant businessman—but that came at a price.

And his mother had paid the price of his fury when she had married for love and not prestige. A price he and his sister were still paying, twelve years after his parents' death, right down to the real reason why he had stolen days away from his team and the frantic lifestyle he had created for himself to come to Kingsmede in the first place.

There could only be one driving goal as far as Leo was concerned.

He was here to do a job and part of that job was honouring his aunt's risk and commitment when she had taken in her orphaned niece and nephew and even found them work in her hotel.

He owed it to her to repay that loyalty with the best work he could do. Of course she had already told him many times that his success in the business world was more than enough reward for any help she had given him.

But that was not how Leo Grainger worked. *Far from it.*

Arabella Rizzi had taught him the most important lesson he had ever learned in his life.

She had told him to respect loyalty and personal integrity more than anything else in this world. So far she had been proven right time and time again and Leo had no intention of changing the way he did business.

His loyalty to his parents went deeper than money or power or reputation—even deeper than his constant drive to maintain control. Grainger Consulting had built up a reputation for being totally objective, and that was precisely what he was going to be now. Objective and focused on the goal—nothing else mattered.

Leo turned away from the house and looked out across the lawns to the trees and open farmland that spread out in all directions around the property.

Sunlit and calm, it was an idyllic setting, if unadventurous.

But what would it be like in winter? On a grey autumn day when the cold wet wind howled across these open fields?

Perhaps the Rizzi team were right? Perhaps an indoor spa extension was the ideal attribute for this small hotel in the middle of the countryside, which could attract visitors winter and summer alike. It certainly needed something to give it an edge.

What could Kingsmede Manor offer him, for example? What was so special about this place that would make him want to choose to come here in the first place and then return time after time? His mission was to find that unique feature which would sell the hotel and keep on selling it.

And the only remarkable thing about Kingsmede Manor that he had seen so far was its previous resident—Sara Fenchurch.

But he had to work fast. His aunt would be flying back to London on Wednesday in time to travel to the Manor and prepare for the meeting on Friday lunchtime. She had asked him to present his recommendations to the whole family. Her family. The Rizzi family. The family who had disowned his mother.

This report was going to have to be spectacular.

He was going to show Paolo Rizzi that he had made the mistake of his life when he had disowned his own daughter and her children.

It was time to show the old man that his grandson was a total professional and that Arabella Rizzi had made the right decision all of those years ago. And Kingsmede Manor was going to be the stage for the big event.

And he was going to be wearing the wedding ring his beloved mother had placed on his father's hand. Oh, yes.

Which brought him right back to the first task of the day.

Leo lifted his head and slid his sunglasses onto his nose.

Time to face the music and find out if Sara Fenchurch had found his father's ring in her bathroom that morning. And eat some humble pie—*his least favourite dish.*

Drat Caspar for setting him up for a blind date in the first place.

Sara had been an astonishing delight until he had opened his big mouth and put his foot in it. Surprising and intriguing and more than just attractive. She had a certain unique quality about her that Leo could not put his finger on and he was kicking himself for being so insensitive.

She certainly would not be hard to find.

The previous evening he had only moonlight and a few fairy lights to guide his way, but this morning he could see that the small wooden gate they'd slipped through the night before was in fact part of a tall red brick wall which formed the boundary to one side of the hotel.

Drawing the gate forward, he stepped through and was immediately on a small lane facing a long low cottage with a red tile roof, square mullioned windows and a low beech hedge providing a barrier to the lane. It was the kind of cottage which would have had a thatched roof when it was built. Flowers spilled out of window boxes, softening the black and white framework and timbered construction.

In the other direction the lane stopped abruptly at a long wooden gate leading to a long orchard. He recognised apples and pears and cherry trees heavy with large red fruits ready to be picked.

But what really caught his attention were the buildings that lay beyond the fruit trees. He had not been able to see them the previous evening but now, rearing up at the end of the cottage garden and extending the full length of the orchard he saw three remarkable ornate glass structures. The closest comparison he could make was to the elaborate hotel palm houses and conservatories he had seen in warmer countries.

Instead of steel structures with thousands of glass panes, these no doubt Victorian designs were white painted wood with ornately carved roof decorations resembling church spires and mediaeval cloisters. These were not greenhouses—these were architectural works of art which called out to his passion for fine design and craftsmanship.

He loved them.

Slightly stunned, Leo strolled across the lane to the gate leading to the painted wooden front entrance of the cottage only a few yards away, complete with pink roses around the door. The picture could have come from a postcard of a classic English scene.

In front of the cottage was a small flower garden about the same size as his car. What it lacked in space it made up for in the exuberance of plants and flowers of every different hue and colour, size and shape which burst out of the small area, creating a riot of pinks and yellows, purples and blues. It was a startling combination and so different in every way from the formal landscaping of the hotel grounds that he could not help but smile. Perhaps this was the precise effect that Sara wanted to create?

Leo stretched out to press the doorbell just as he noticed that a piece of pink fluorescent paper had been taped onto the door. Someone had written in large letters: *'Direct sales to the public. Buy your orchids straight from the greenhouse. Turn right for Cottage Orchids.'*

The notice had not been there last night!

Caspar had told him that Sara grew orchids, but he was not expecting her to grow them at the bottom of her garden! Surely orchids were imported from tropical countries and she would simply have a wholesale warehouse?

Following the instructions, Leo strolled around the corner, followed the length of the cottage wall and directly in front of him was the first of the ornate conservatory greenhouses with a totally charming wooden chalet guarding the entrance. A white hand-painted sign on the wall of the log cabin told him that he had reached Cottage Orchids, Kingsmede Manor. The door was locked but in front of him was the entrance to the greenhouses and as he peered through the glass he saw a hint of movement inside. The door was slightly ajar and, with a small tap on the frame, Leo opened the door and slipped inside the most remarkable room he had ever been in.

Stretched out in long rows were waist-high wooden racks covered with plants, not in a random pattern, but in strict order by colour and size. Directly in front of him and along one side of the building were pale colours. White, ivory, cream and every shade of gold and yellow. As he stepped closer he realised that all of the plants in this room had the same kind of leaf and flower. The flower shapes and types of blossom were all the same, no matter what colour they were.

So this was a specialist nursery! Niche marketing. Clever. Someone had done their homework. He liked that.

A narrow footpath the width of one paving slab separated those plants from the middle row, where the colours were pinks, oranges and stunning apricots. Young plants, old plants, small plants and tall plants were arranged in strict order with scarcely space between them for the tiny transparent plastic plant pots holding their roots, which spilled out in green and grey tendrils over the surface of each container.

He looked over to the other side of the greenhouse to what must be a nursery area with baby plants in tiny pots as well as plants with stubby sticks sticking out from the compost. It seemed as though every inch of racking space was covered with orchid plants of one type or another.

A distinctive sound caught his ears. Somewhere a girl was singing along in snatches to a pop song with a very sweet voice.

Leo looked around the edge of the staging and shook his head, scarcely believing what he was looking at, and smiled across at Sara Fenchurch. It was the first time that he had smiled that day—but he had good reason.

Sara was nodding her head from side to side as she sang to herself. And it looked as if she was giving a plant a sponge bath.

It was probably the biggest orchid plant he had ever seen, with long thick green fleshy leaves. And she was sponging each leaf in turn underneath and on top. Her hands moved in slow languorous strokes, sensually caressing the leaves one after another with infinite care and with such loving attention that Leo's blood pounded just a little hotter.

At her feet a golden-coloured cat was stretched out so that the sun could warm his tummy on the bright sunlit floor. The cat's eyes were closed but as Leo stepped forward he raised his head just enough to look at him, yawned, stretched out a little longer, then went back to sleep again.

The radio was blasting out modern pop music, lively and fun, so that it was not surprising that Sara had not heard him come into the room, offering him the opportunity to observe her at close range.

Of course he could have interrupted her—but this was a totally self indulgent pleasure he wanted to stretch out for as long as he could. Especially when their next conversation might not be so cordial.

Sara was wearing a yellow T-shirt advertising a brand of orchid compost, green capri pants and spotty fabric plimsolls.

It was strange how this colourful and totally unlikely ensemble only seemed to make her lovely figure even more attractive.

This version of Sara was a revelation. Entrancing and natural.

As he watched in silence and appreciation, she gently lifted the orchid plant away onto a draining board and popped a collection of what looked to Leo like clear plastic food tubs into her sink. Her hands were in constant motion scrubbing and washing the tiny containers as she focused her total attention on the simple task.

An orange baseball cap covered her short brown hair and shaded her eyes from the light streaming in from the long window in front of the sink but he could see a sprinkle of freckles across her lightly tanned nose and cheeks.

The elegant woman he had met the previous evening was gone, replaced by a slim girl in working clothes who seemed to take great delight in scrubbing out plant pots on a hot Sunday morning. She did not need make-up or expensive clothing or accessories to look stunning—she was lovely just as she was.

The smart city girl in the slick black costume he had met last night he could deal with, but this version of Sara Fenchurch was far more unexpected.

Helen and Caspar were wealthy and successful, with lives in the fast lane of London society. That was the world where Leo had made his business—so who was this girl who chose to spend a hot Sunday morning washing plant pots? Was this her plant nursery? Was she an employee of some bigger company? He should have asked Caspar a lot more questions before they'd left this morning—background information was always useful for negotiations, and suddenly he felt out of place. This was Sara's territory—not his. The pretty girl in a T-shirt who looked absurdly cute might not be so generous when she remembered how he had slighted her the night before.

Either way, he was standing here in a black business suit and black shirt on a summer day, feeling completely overdressed, while she was comfortable and cool in her work clothes. He had rarely felt so out of his depth, or so attracted to a girl who was totally natural and comfortable in her own skin—and what skin!

That kind of combination would spell trouble if he stayed around long enough to get to know her better—she was dynamite with a slow burning fuse.

Leo was still trying to formulate some way of introducing himself without looking like a complete idiot when she turned around, saw him and dropped the pots back into the sink with a clatter and then a splosh when they hit the water.

'Good morning, Miss Fenchurch,' he announced calmly with a half smile on his face. 'I'm sorry if I startled you but there was no answer at the cabin.'

She looked up at him wide-eyed, then turned away and rested her hand against the sink. 'Not a problem, Mr Grainger. No problem at all. Are you interested in buying an orchid?' She gestured over one shoulder. 'As you can see, I have a wide selection in an assortment of colours.'

And then she looked up at him through her eyelashes and, as their eyes met, he knew that she was already two steps ahead of him. She knew who he was, why he was there and had absolutely no intention of letting him get away with anything.

He paused and nodded. 'Actually, I have come

to apologise for ruining our pleasant evening—then I'm going to buy an orchid. Is that better?'

Sara twitched her lips and tilted her head slightly in his direction but turned back to her pots and kept on scrubbing and rinsing and scrubbing. Only when she had drained every single one of the pots did she slip off her rubber gloves and turn fully towards him with her back against the sink.

Leo braced himself. He deserved whatever was coming his way. Which was why when she did speak what she said knocked him more than he could have imagined.

'Is that why you recommended me to the hotel? To make up for your comments about the blind date you were so pleased to have escaped?'

He winced and gave her a brief nod. There was no point in denying it. 'Partly that,' he admitted, 'and I do apologise for insulting you in any way. I really did have no idea that you were the girl that Helen had asked me to meet.'

And then he took a breath. He had indulged himself far too long—time was money. Down to business. 'But there is something else. I believe I left my ring in your bathroom last night and I would like to have it back, please. That ring means a lot to me.'

'Of course. I understand,' she said and opened her mouth to say something else, then hesitated and seemed to change her mind and simply shook her head. 'And I do appreciate what you did for me. Thank you. It's a great opportunity and I have every intention of taking up the offer. I want you to know that the Manor can rely on me completely. Even if there is a *slight* delay while I make alternative arrangements. But I will do it. I will find a way of making it possible. It simply will take longer than I had expected. That's all.'

Leo was close enough to hear the trembling in her voice and he took a step forward, his hand resting gently on one edge of the wooden staging.

'A delay?' he asked and glanced around. 'The hotel manager was very interested and you certainly seem to have plenty of plants to sell. Assuming that these are your plants.'

She gave a half chuckle. 'Oh, yes. All mine. And there are two more greenhouses this size outside. I may have plants at the moment, but...' And then she swallowed and seemed to struggle with the words. Then she really did have problems talking and turned away from him and rested her hands on the edge of the sink so tightly that her knuckles were white but the stress was only too obvious in the tone of her voice.

'I heard the bad news about the hotel expansion plans this morning,' she went on as though she were talking to some imaginary figure on the other side of the glass, then gave a half smile as the radio belted out a lively dance track. 'So I have been trying to cheer myself up. Without much success. At this precise moment I am... going through my options but, rest assured, the Rizzi Hotel group will have my proposals on Friday as promised.'

Leo covered the few steps that separated them so that he was standing next to her, looking into her face. She was blinking hard and clearly distressed about something.

'A luxury spa will create jobs for local people, and bring new investment into Kingsmede,' he replied in the low consolatory voice he had perfected for speeches where he had to spell out the hard facts. 'It could bring a lot more guests to the hotel, which means more opportunity for you to sell your flowers. I'm not sure how that equates to bad news.'

Instantly her shoulders dropped back and she turned her head around and looked straight into his eyes.

'In that case you clearly do not have even the remotest idea what this spa extension means to my business,' she said in a low calm voice, but her gaze stayed fixed, her eyes locked onto his.

Until now he had thought that her eyes were

brown but in the warm sunlight he was so captivated by a pair of dark green eyes flecked with amber and milk chocolate flakes that he had to blink several times and break their connection so that he could focus on what had shaken her so very badly.

'Then tell me,' he replied with a slight nod in her direction, his upper body leaning slightly forward in encouragement.

Sara gave a brief nod. 'Okay. I will. Look around, Mr Grainger. What do you see?'

Leo glanced from side to side. 'A stunning glasshouse full of orchids?' Then he smiled back at her. 'And it's Leo. Please.'

Sara lifted her chin. 'Very well. Leo. You're right. It is stunning and I am lucky to have it. The floor we are standing on and this beautiful greenhouse came with the cottage.' Then she turned away from him again and looked out of the window before she continued. 'My grandmother also left me the other two greenhouses but they stand on a piece of land I rent from my neighbour.'

She waved her hand towards the high red brick wall to her right. 'All of this area as far as the wall used to be the kitchen gardens of the house. The high wall was the south-facing boundary of the gardens. My grandmother had to sell this land to pay to repair the roof about ten years ago and had always intended to buy it back again, but it never happened and she died before she could do anything about it.'

A long slow sigh was followed by a sharp intake of breath before she was ready to carry on, as though she had to prepare herself to say the words. 'I found out this morning that the organic farmer who bought the land all of those years ago has just received an offer from the hotel which will make it possible for him to retire. He can't afford to turn it down but was sworn to secrecy until the hotel was ready to go public. And now they have.'

Sara reached into the pocket of her trousers and pulled out a slim brown envelope. 'The official notice was waiting for me in the post.' Then she pressed her lips together and shrugged. 'You are probably used to seeing small businesses go to the wall for the sake of increased profits for the Rizzi Hotel chain but you'll excuse me if I take a more selfish view.'

Leo looked at her for a few seconds and recognised that look on her face only too well. He had seen it on the faces of his clients too many times not to know what shock and dismay looked like. The last thing this girl needed was some foolish man asking about a ring left in her bathroom.

Then he gave himself a mental shake. Snap

out of it! His dad's ring was the only thing that he was interested in. That was why he was here. *Wasn't it?*

Then his brain caught up with what she had said. And he almost winced in recognition that she was right about that, if nothing else. There were countless small suppliers and support staff that were casualties of the big company mergers and acquisitions he advised on every day of the week. But they were not his problem and never could be.

His clients paid him very well to give them an objective assessment of what needed to be done to increase company profitability. That was his speciality. Not sentimental consideration of the individual business owners who would have to go through what Sara was about to face. That was not his job.

Of course he never got to meet the many small businesses face to face or even know their names. Why should he? Unlike now, when the girl he had been dancing with the night before was fighting to hold back tears, with an uncertain future ahead of her. And all because of his aunt's drive to increase turnover at the Manor.

Suddenly the collar of his black fitted shirt felt tight on his neck, and he shuffled uncomfortably inside his summer-weight cashmere wool jacket. Sun was streaming into the hot and humid orchid house and he had rarely felt so awkward or out of his comfort zone. This was one spot where he did not have the clothing or the attitude to fit the environment. A hostile takeover of two international companies was nothing compared to actually being in the same small space as someone who was reeling from the impact of a chain of events set in motion by Rizzi management months earlier, someone who owned a business his aunt would never have even heard of.

She dropped the envelope onto the draining board, not caring that it would be soaked. 'I have been stupid and naive. I am probably not making much sense this morning. This news is all still very new to me and I'm having a problem working out where I go from here.'

Sara blinked several times and wiped a very grubby finger under her eyes and gave him a half smile. 'I accept your apology, and thank you for coming in person, but it might be better if you left now.'

Then she lifted her head and gave him something close to a scowl. 'From what Tony Evans told me, you are part of the Rizzi family who have just bought me out,' she whispered, her mouth tight and thin with suppressed feeling. 'I know that you are Caspar's friend but I have a great deal to think about and would appreciate being left alone to get on with sorting my business out. So thank you and have a nice day. Life. Whatever.'

And, before Leo could reply or react, she grabbed the nearest pale yellow orchid plant, which was about three feet tall and bursting with huge blossoms, and thrust it at his black jacket and shirt with such vigour that the only thing that he could do was grab hold of it before it caused serious damage.

He had only just clasped it against the front of his jacket when she slipped behind him on the narrow walkway, giving him a waft of floral scent and bleach mixed with warm girl, and grabbed hold of both of his shoulders with hands which were probably grubbier than he was used to, and physically turned him around to face the entrance.

The next thing he knew, Leo was standing outside the greenhouse cuddling a yellow orchid in a transparent pot and not entirely sure how he'd got there.

CHAPTER FIVE

S<small>ARA</small> stumbled down the centre of the green-house as best she could, her head dazed from all that had happened in her normally tranquil life in the past twenty-four hours.

She really could not handle any more surprises today—all she wanted to do was block out the effects of the shocking news she'd received and seeing Leo again in daylight, and liking him even more, with hard physical work.

There were people relying on her to deliver their orchids. That was what she had to focus on now—getting through one day at a time, and somehow, along the way, she would come up with a brilliant idea about how to get out of this mess.

Her hands stilled on the cool ceramic of the sink.

But of course there was no way out.

If the land was sold, then the hotel would want to use every square inch of the expensive real estate they had invested in. She could hardly blame the elderly farmer she had known most of her life for taking a chance to retire in comfort with his family when he was offered it.

And of course the hotel did not want only the kitchen gardens—oh, no, they wanted another ten acres of his land as well. For car parks.

Car parks! In a few months her cottage garden would be backing onto tarmac car parks.

Sara pushed away from the sink and walked slowly down to the side exit of the cool green-house, carefully drew open the door and walked the few steps towards the hotter and more humid tropical orchid house. She reached out a hand to-wards the door and then let it fall away, stepped back and looked around, content to simply enjoy this stunning place which she loved so much.

The high brick wall of the hotel which had once been her home was on one side, the curved walls designed to retain the heat of the fruit trees which were still trained against the surface. Apples and pears. Turkish figs. All so delicious when they were picked straight from the tree.

It had been her grandmother's idea to put the orchid houses on the opposite west-facing side of the kitchen garden so that she could control the light but still have the heat for most of the day, and this was where she had spent so many of her final years, just pottering around, enjoying the plants that she had treasured and created. A vegetable plot for one person did not make much sense, but orchids had been her passion. She'd even admitted over one too many glasses of sherry one Christmas that she sometimes preferred her orchids to people.

Orchids did not let her down, or run away, or desert their families when they needed them.

Oh, Nana!

Car parks. They would probably knock down the old walls to make a direct link to the main hotel building through this space, then onto the fields. Tearing away centuries of heritage at the same time.

What did they care about that? This was a business, after all. No room for sentimental nonsense about the past and the people who had created these buildings and cared for them with such love over the generations.

Her eyes fluttered closed and she sniffed away a rising swell of panic. No. This was not the end. It could not be the end. Not after three years of relentless work.

She was so preoccupied with thoughts and concerns that the sound of footsteps at the door barely registered until she heard the greenhouse door creak open behind her.

Trying to fix a smile on her face, Sara turned

back towards the entrance, then jumped, surprised to see Leo only a few feet away. Her
shoulders slumped in startled surprise.

'Oh, please do not make this any more difficult than it already is,' she said to Leo, who was
leaning casually against the door frame simply
watching her in silence.

Last night, in his costume and under the
moonlight, she could not have imagined that
he could be more handsome or more attractive,
but the soft sunlight infused his Mediterranean
complexion with an entrancing glow that high-
lighted his natural tan and made the smile lines
around his mouth and the corners of his eyes
even more attractive.

He had a mouth designed for smiling. Those
blue-grey eyes were so mesmerising that she
could barely look at him without remembering
the touch of his hand at her waist and how it felt
to be swept along in the glorious waltz they had
shared the previous evening.

For a few minutes she had felt like a normal
girl out on a normal date with a normal guy and
had actually dared to enjoy herself—until he
had brought her crashing back down to earth
by reminding her that she had been set up by
Helen on a blind date. With the bloke who had
no desire whatsoever of going out with his
friend's school pal.

And she had been right back where she always was. Last of the line when it came to being picked for anything.

She had been so humiliated even before she'd realised that he had seen her underwear and the turmoil inside her simple one-bedroomed cottage.

And now here he was, looking slick as a slick thing from slick land while she was... Who she was.

It was a shame that her poor treacherous body refused to ignore the fact that she was staring at the way the fine silky fabric of his fitted black shirt was stretched across a broad muscular chest—and liked it far too much for comfort.

She could not like him. She dare not like this strange alien creature who had just arrived from outer space to appear in her little world.

A slim tailored black suit and fitted black shirt was just about the most inappropriate clothing she could have chosen for any guest to come to a plant nursery and yet somehow he managed to look cool, contained and sophisticated. An elegant man used to an elegant lifestyle and elegant people in elegant surroundings. So what was he doing here with her?

Ah, of course—the ring! She had not given Leo his ring back! And from the determined look on his face he was not going to go without it. Leo Grainger could have invented the expression 'stiff upper lip'.

Pity that his plump lower lip was trying to smile and not succeeding. He must be hot under all of that black clothing in the warm sunshine but he didn't show it. The top two buttons of his black silk shirt were undone, revealing a hint of tanned chest and the possibility of chest hair. No doubt there was some beautiful fashion model-cum-personal assistant waiting for him back in London whose job it was to admire that broad muscular chest on a daily basis.

It was a tough job but someone had to do it, she supposed.

Perhaps she could go on a waiting list?

It was strange how the longer she felt him watching her, the warmer she became. A blush of heat burst up to her neck and she quickly turned away, back to the work in hand.

She was not allowed to stare at his chest or any other part of his anatomy, for that matter. Shame on her! Crushes of all kinds were for teenagers, not grown women, especially when she had only known him a few hours.

For all she knew, he could have found out the previous evening who she was from Caspar or Helen when he'd rejoined the party.

That must have come as a shock.

For a tiny fraction of a second she almost felt

sorry for him, but then she remembered her humiliation and embarrassment and lifted her chin defiantly.

This was the man who was working for the hotel management who were going to evict her!

'Have you forgotten something?' she asked and blinked several times, content to watch his exasperated expression for a few seconds before the pale grey-blue eyes narrowed ever so slightly. 'Or have you come back to gloat about how your family are just about to put me out of business?'

Leo cleared his throat. 'Yes to the first question but no to the second. It's been a while since someone escorted me off their premises and I have to confess that I am not sure I like it.'

'Oh, I have every confidence that you will soon recover,' she said in a low voice and gave him a very brittle smile. 'I'm sure you appreciate that I am pretty busy trying to save what I can right now, so have a good trip back to London.'

She raised one hand and gestured over Leo's shoulder. 'And please close the door on your way out.'

'Not so fast. You seem to have all the answers,' Leo replied with a tilt of his head while the rest of him stayed stubbornly where it was, totally ignoring her. 'Except that you may not have all of the facts,' he added, folding his arms and looking down his long straight nose at her with a fierce sparkle in his eyes which was no doubt intended to pressurise business executives, and any female in sight, into total submission.

She should detest him for how effective it was, but instead she took the hit by locking her wobbly knees and breathing a little slower to calm her racing heart.

'Okay, I confess,' he said and pressed one hand flat against his chest. 'I did recommend your plant nursery to the hotel in the vain hope that it would act as a small form of apology, but I was happy to do so. I've known Caspar long enough to trust his judgement, even if it did mean putting my neck and my reputation on the block. And who is Tony Evans, by the way?'

Sara knew that she should leave this conversation alone and get back to work. All of her instincts started screaming and ringing alarm bells, warning her not to get involved by asking for more information, but she could not help it.

'Tony is the Events Manager at the hotel,' she answered meekly, only too aware that he was using this side question to deflect her from the true enormity of the problems. 'I went looking for more work there today and he mentioned that you had recommended my nursery and—'

she paused and shrugged her shoulders '—he might have mentioned that you are related to the owners of the hotel. And apparently you are a mega business consultant.'

'Ah—' he nodded knowingly '—I only dealt with the hotel manager, not his team. And you added two and two together and came up with five? Is that about right? Well, at least some of that is correct. Yes, my aunt is one of the Rizzi family who bought this house three years ago from your family,' he said. 'But I actually have my own business consultancy—which has nothing to do with the Rizzi Hotel chain. Sorry to disappoint you but I am not on the hotel payroll.'

'Oh. So you don't work for Kingsmede Manor?'

Leo shook his head very slowly from side to side.

'And you didn't have anything to do with the decision to buy the old kitchen garden?'

His reply was a slight nod in her direction, combined with a killer smile. 'Nothing at all. That decision would have been taken months ago by senior management.'

'Oh. Okay. I always have had a vivid imagination,' she admitted with a tiny shoulder shrug. 'Especially when I feel sorry for myself. Which is not very often,' she hastened to add. 'It's just that I don't get out very often and every waking moment of the last three years has been spent building up these three greenhouses to the point where I can start to think about making improvements. This is my world and it means everything to me.' And then she shut up, realising that she was giving far too much away. 'And I'm rambling. Sorry—I don't usually tell my problems to a complete stranger.'

Her head dropped and she focused her eyes on the sunlight on the stone flagstones, which was why it came as a total shock when his forefinger pressed against her chin and tipped it up towards him.

'Hardly a stranger,' he said with a gentle smile. 'We have our own song and everything. We even like the same chocolates. Besides—' and he dropped his hand and rested it lightly on her arm '—according to Helen, we are perfect for each other, and who am I to argue with such a higher force? Oh—and there is something you should know. I do not gloat. Ever.'

'You should gloat. Seriously. I have no idea why Helen thinks that we are in the least compatible. Apparently you are a famous business consultant—' and she gestured towards him with one hand, then flipped it over to point to her chest '—while I have a business which just started going downhill fast. Not a happy comparison. Let's just say that I suspected a heavy amount of guilt was involved in your decision to recommend me. Oh—and a burning desire to get your ring back.'

Sara could not help it. Her mouth twisted into a grin. 'No, I hadn't forgotten about it. I was going to bring it up to the hotel later,' and then she winced sharply as Leo moved his fingers over the scratches on her arm that Pasha had given her the evening before.

He gasped and looked down at the inside of her arm and the line of red scratch marks. 'What happened to you? Did you burn yourself? Or was it an attack of the killer mutant orchids?'

'Not at all.' Sara laughed. 'Did you see that giant lazy cat of mine? My boy might be an old man in cat years but he can still wield a mighty scratch.' And then she shrugged slightly. 'I'm allergic to cat hair so when Pasha scratches me I have to put up with an itchy red arm for a couple of days. I got away with it last night by taking a couple of allergy tablets, which was probably not a good idea combined with Caspar's special cocktail.'

Sara lifted her right hand to waist height palm side up, fluttered her fingers and then flipped it over and brought it sharply down towards her knees. 'I crashed out when I got back to the cottage, didn't I? I blame Caspar for the whole thing.'

Leo raised his eyebrows. 'You wouldn't be

the only person.' And he looked at her with soft eyes. 'Why do you have a cat if you're allergic to cat hair? I can't quite understand the logic in that.'

'Pasha belonged to my grandmother and was thirteen years young when she passed away. Nobody else would take a cat that age and I promised my grandmother that I would give him a home. And that's it. I now have an elderly tomcat for a pet. He is good company, actually, even if he is hopeless when it comes to catching mice these days.'

Sara peered through the glass to Pasha, who was still stretched out in the sunshine with his tail flicking up now and again to indicate he was dreaming. But when she looked back towards Leo she was taken aback by the expression on his face.

'What is it?' she asked softly and their eyes met. For a fleeting second she felt as though he was looking at her as if he was seeing her for the first time. He had a look in those blue-grey eyes with that certain something that, in another time and another place, she could almost have said was interest.

Or was he more interested in her old cat and her sob story? Both of them pathetic and both of them on their way out, in one way or another.

Lovely. He must be so impressed!

'Don't you dare feel sorry for me,' she snorted before he had a chance to answer. 'I chose to give Pasha a home. I chose to invest everything I have in these orchid houses, even though I am only renting this piece of land. My decision, for better or worse—' and then she faltered '—no matter how dim that looks right now.'

'I didn't say a word,' he retorted and raised both hands in surrender, before dropping them back onto his hips.

'You don't have to. I know that I must seem totally pathetic. Gloat away.'

And then he did something which totally knocked the wind from her sails and the air from her lungs.

He pushed away from the greenhouse door, reached forward and took both of her hands in his so that her fingers were completely encased inside his palms.

She was so startled that she didn't have time to pull away before he was in her personal space and talking in a low intense voice and those stunning blue-grey eyes were focused totally on hers, making it absolutely impossible for her to look away.

'You are not pathetic,' he said in a clear, calm voice, as refreshing as a waft of cool air on a hot afternoon. 'And I do not feel sorry for you. On the contrary, I admire you for making a decision and sticking to it. You made a promise to someone you cared about and you did that knowing that it could cause you problems. That is something you should be proud of.'

He admired her? Was this some sort of joke?

Sara looked deeper into his eyes and saw only sincerity that brought a lump to her throat and the blood thumping in her chest.

'But you were looking at me as though I had two heads a minute ago,' she replied in a low voice which was a lot more unsteady than she would have liked.

'Let's just say that not many people surprise me these days,' he replied with a smile. 'I admire loyalty in anyone, especially if it costs them. Okay?' And then his voice softened to match his sweet smile. 'Okay?' he asked again.

Her shoulders seemed to drop ten inches just at the sound of his voice. Perhaps Leo should go into the massage business?

'Okay,' she replied with a tilt of her head, 'and thank you. I'm not used to being admired, so it has come as a bit of shock. Especially on top of the bad news about the land sale.'

Then she flung back her head and dared to chuckle as the irony of the situation hit her. She was holding hands with a dazzling, handsome man with eyes the colour of a winter sky while her plant nursery was just about to go to the wall.

'Do you know the funny thing? Cottage Orchids has actually been shortlisted for an award. Can you believe that? An award for my entrepreneurial skills.' Her right hand slid out from Leo's hand and traced the letters in the air above their heads. 'Local Businesswoman of the Year.' Then she dropped her hand onto her hip and gave him a tiny shrug. 'What a joke. I could use some serious business advice myself right now. If only I could afford to pay for…it.' Then she froze mid-sentence.

Leo was a mega business consultant.

She needed a business consultant.

And she needed one badly.

And he did have a point about Helen. Her friend would never have arranged a blind date unless she thought that she and Leo could get along.

But that would mean asking for help. And even the thought of asking this Adonis of a man to give his time and energy as a favour made her teeth go on edge and she cringed inside.

Worse—he was part of the Rizzi family! How could she possibly trust him to give her impartial advice? No. It was impossible.

Especially when she still had his precious ring in her pocket.

Her mind raced. Oh, no, she could not do that! She could not hold his property to ransom.

That would be totally wrong, not to say unethical. And he was Caspar's friend, after all.

Desperate times called for desperate measures. She had been out here working for two hours and the only ideas she had come up with to save her business were too long-term to be any use at all over the next few weeks before she had to pack up everything she could save.

His professional advice could make a difference and at that particular moment she needed all the help she could get.

All she had to do was forget the fact that he was a professional business guru who probably charged his clients the earth for the benefit of his advice, and swallow her pride and just ask him.

She could do this.

She could humiliate herself yet again.

She chewed at her lower lip, aware that he was looking at her with his eyebrows creased together, clearly bewildered at this strange woman who had been trying to get rid of him. Perhaps she could put it down to mood swings? That always confused boys.

'Look, Leo. It's like this.' She took a deep breath and blurted out her question before she could change her mind. 'I need a business consultant. You are a business consultant. It seems to me to point one way.'

Then she smiled sweetly at him, slipped her hand from his, reached into her trouser pocket and waved his ring between two fingers.

'I was going to give you your ring back this afternoon, but now I would like to offer you a trade. You can have your ring back in exchange for a few hours' work. Ten hours at most—even quicker if you really put your mind to my problems.'

She held up one hand when he started to bluster in protest. 'I know that your family own the hotel and I know that there is no way I can prevent the land from being sold. That ship has sailed. So I am not asking you to do anything that could harm your family.'

Then her hand dropped and she smiled through clenched teeth and looked up sheepishly into Leo's startled face. 'All I need is a second opinion about what I can do to make the best of this situation and save my business. Right now, I have no clue about the options I have and I am in great danger of losing everything. That's all I need—some advice about my options. It won't take long, and I would really appreciate it. So. What do you say? Want to make a trade? Your time for the ring. It's quite simple, really.'

Simple? Leo choked on the words that were bursting to the surface and stared open-mouthed at Sara, who was just standing there smiling at him in her prettiest, cheekiest, freckliest fashion as though she had just invited him for afternoon tea.

His situation was anything but *simple.*

He couldn't give this girl advice without compromising his position—but he also could not tell her that he was on assignment for his aunt.

He had given his word that he would keep this project a secret.

He had just told her that he was not an employee of the hotel chain, and that was true—he was doing this work for his aunt as a personal favour.

His aunt was the only one of his mother's Rizzi family who had reached out to him and his sister and offered practical help when their parents had died in a road accident. He owed her. And he would keep his reason for staying on at the hotel to himself, even if it meant being less than honest with Sara.

He had walked away from the Rizzi Hotel chain a long time ago and had absolutely no intention of ever joining the payroll. Not while his grandfather was in control.

And nothing—*nothing*—was going to come between him and his mission here.

Not even a pretty girl who was so cheeky that she somehow believed that he could simply drop everything else in his life and give her his undivided personal attention in exchange for the return of his own property!

She had no idea what she was asking.

There was a waiting list of companies who were willing to pay top rates for this kind of advice, and it had taken a lot of juggling to squeeze these few days away from the office into his schedule. He had a mountain of paperwork and emails and reports to finish back at the hotel. There was no way he could take so much time away from his core business and current projects to help Sara.

Of course, they were not friends of friends who had struck rock bottom and were as intriguing as Sara Fenchurch—but it was still a lot to ask.

So where did that leave him? *He had to have that ring back. And fast.*

He raised an eyebrow. 'You want *me* to give *you* business advice in exchange for my own ring. Is that right?'

'Don't put it like that,' she said. 'It makes me sound as though I might be…well…an opportunist. Instead of just foolish and desperate. With an old cat to support,' she added in a rush.

'Oh, well,' he replied. 'That makes all the difference. How could I possibly forget about the cat?'

He lowered his head and glared at Sara down his nose in a very half-hearted attempt to intimidate her. 'I could always complain to Helen and Caspar that you are holding my property to ransom. I think that they would take a very dim view of that kind of behaviour.'

She sniffed and shook her head from side to side. Then she raised her eyebrows and grinned cheekily. 'You wouldn't. You like Caspar. And Helen is my best friend in the whole world.'

Sara gave a short shrug. 'It would be such a shame if Caspar's life was a misery because you could not spare a few hours of your time to give some business advice to a lady in distress. How could you be so ungallant?'

And then she sniffed and reached into her pocket for her mobile phone. 'Why don't I give Helen a call now and ask her to turn the car around because I've had bad news about my business? Of course I haven't told her yet because I didn't want to upset her so close to the wedding, but seeing as I'm all alone and broke…'

Leo's hand came up and his fingers closed over the open cell phone. 'You didn't tell Helen when you heard your bad news this morning?'

She stuck her neck out and hissed in disbelief. 'Are you kidding? She would have dropped everything and stayed here to try and sort things out. I couldn't do that to her. Not when her wedding is only four weeks away and she is meeting Caspar's parents this afternoon to go through the final plans. She has enough to worry about. No—' and she stood back and dropped her voice '—I have to work through the next steps on my own. When I have something concrete to tell her, then yes, I will talk it through, but until then I would prefer to keep this to myself.'

She looked into his face for a second and frowned. 'You're giving me that two headed look again. Now what have I done?'

'More what you haven't done.' He lifted his head, sighed out loud, then nodded. 'Just how alone and broke are you? Because, coming from a girl who used to live in that house—' and he nodded over his shoulder towards the hotel '—you will forgive me if my idea of being broke is slightly different from yours.'

There was a sharp intake of breath and she stared at him wide-eyed. 'I don't believe it. You actually think that just because my grandmother left my mother a huge house that there was money in the family? Oh, dear. Another bubble for me to burst.'

Then she shook her head slowly from side to side. 'Huge debts we knew nothing about, followed by even bigger repair bills. Don't even talk about the tax. All of which means that I have no employees and no backup team. Cottage Orchids is what you see in front of you. There is me, the cat and a cheap delivery van. Everything I have earned has been ploughed back into the business. I have some savings, which had been intended to pay the rent, but that is it. That's why I have to resort to these sorts of tactics to persuade you to help me out. Otherwise, these glasshouses are going to *collapse* around me and I won't be able to do anything about it. I will lose everything.'

Lose everything. Leo bit the inside of his cheek. *Why did she have to use that particular expression?*

Grainger Consulting dealt with companies large enough to survive in one way or another even without his intervention, but to lose everything?

There was no way that Sara could know that she had just described his own personal nightmare made real, and the words rebounded inside his head.

He had fought long and hard to make sure that he would never, ever face the horror of losing everything again. He had checked his investment and property portfolio only that morning and, if he wanted to, he need never work again.

And it did not make one bit of difference. The fear was still there.

He inhaled slowly through his nose, anxious not to show Sara the impact of her innocent and totally open and honest statement. No complicated risk assessment needed here. She slouched casually against the glasshouse, looking at him with her hopeful lopsided grin as the sunlight brought out the freckles on her chin. Everything about this girl, who was pinning her hopes and dreams on him, of all people, screamed out to him that she knew as much about business management as he knew about orchid propagation. And she was asking him to help her. One to one.

He swallowed down something close to personal concern, and then sniffed it away. What a ridiculous notion. He did not do sentiment. He did objective analysis based on data.

Perhaps Sara did need someone like him to look at her options. But it would have to be done professionally. Advising a one woman plant business would be easy enough—if she was prepared to accept some hard facts.

There was a long pause before Leo lifted his chin.

'I'm beginning to get the picture. And you accept the fact that the Rizzi Hotel group is not going to walk away from buying the land? Nothing is going to change that fact.'

Her shoulders slumped and she seemed to falter and swallow down what he sincerely prayed was not the start of tears, before biting her lower lip and nodding once for emphasis before flicking back her head and glaring defiantly at him. 'Yes, I accept that my business is toast and I am going to be evicted. Can we move on now?'

'One more question. Have you ever had any kind of business or marketing advice at all?' he asked.

Her face seemed to relax a little at his first sign that he might actually be thinking about her proposal. 'No, but I can learn. Do you really think that will help me save my nursery?'

Not completely convinced that he was doing the right thing, even as he spoke, Leo reluctantly gave his terms. 'I can't promise you that—but I can talk you through some options. What you do with them has to be your decision, not mine. As you say, you have to choose the direction you want to go in. All I can do is give you a few maps to help you to decide.'

'Maps. I like the sound of that! Because I have to tell you, Leo, that at the moment I am feeling totally lost. I may need guidebooks as well.' She exhaled with a slow sigh. 'You might as well know that I hate asking anyone for help. Anyone. Which makes it extra hard for me to ask you to give me some advice. I wouldn't do it at all unless I was seriously desperate and it's

important to me that you know that. Just so that
we are clear.'

Leo fought back a smile. Perhaps they had a
lot more in common than he had ever expected.
To feel as if the whole world was against you
and there was nowhere to go and nobody to
help? Oh, yes, he knew what that felt like.

But, as he looked at Sara, the small begin-
nings of an idea crept into his mind.

He had one objective here at Kingsmede
Manor and that was to find some way to give
this hotel a competitive edge. And who better
could there be to give him the inside story about
the place than the girl who had lived there most
of her life? She had twenty plus years of background and insider information about this hotel
which he could use—if he could persuade her to
tell him. While keeping his assignment a secret.

Yes, it would be a deception of sorts. But he
couldn't afford to get sentimental and it was
Sara who had suggested it. She stood to gain
just as much as he did.

If he made sure that she never found out that
he was there to help out the very family who
were putting her business at risk.

Which was probably why the words came
out of his mouth before his brain had properly
engaged.

'I was planning to stay at the hotel for a day

or two. I suppose I could give you a few hours of my time tomorrow morning. Just to take a look at your business strategy and work through some options. How does that sound?'

'A few hours?' she gasped in disbelief and waved her arms about. 'I am going to need more than a few hours! I have to save my entire family heritage here!'

'That's my offer,' he said, unmoved.

'What else can I offer you in exchange for some extra time?' she asked with a smile. 'Crash course in orchid cultivation? Budding for beginners? Or perhaps your lady friends could use an orchid in their lives? Girls love flowers and my special hybrids smell really wonderful. The girls will love you for ever.'

And that really did make him laugh out loud. 'Well, I might just take you up on your kind offer but not at the moment, thanks. However—' and he hesitated with a twinge of guilt as another far more pressing excuse for being with Sara kicked in '—there is something you could help me with. I am interested in Kingsmede Manor. Call it professional curiosity if you will, but the history behind a country house like this and the people who designed it and lived in it has always fascinated me.'

Now that was true. He *did* have a personal interest in the design aspects of the property.

'The Manor? You do realise that once you get me talking about the house you would never be able to shut me up? But yes, of course, if you're interested I've inherited a lot of material about the history of the house and you are welcome to look at it. But you do realise that an exclusive viewing of these historical documents will cost you a lot more than a few hours of your business time?'

'How about four hours a day for the next three days?' Leo replied and held back a laugh as Sara's mouth fell open in surprise. But then she pulled herself back together and held out her hand, clearly anxious to grab his offer before he had a chance to think about it and change his mind. 'Done. Do we have a deal?'

'Deal.' He nodded and they shook on it. Her hand was warm and small, but her handshake was solid. It was the handshake of someone who meant what they said, and the prospect of spending a lot more time in Sara's company suddenly seemed like the best decision that *he* had made all day.

'So how soon can you get changed?' she asked. 'I can be ready in about an hour. Oh, and one word of advice. Don't wear black. The compost gets everywhere.'

'Oh, no,' Leo replied in a slow languorous voice. 'I only come in one colour and that colour is black. And I start tomorrow morning. Take it or leave it.'

And he gave her that half smile that brought a bright flush to her cheeks for all of the ten seconds it took her to say, 'I'll take it. I will definitely take it.'

CHAPTER SIX

LEO swiped his thumb across the display on his personal organiser as he strolled across the stone patio outside Kingsmede Manor and checked down the list of emails which had come in from the project team leaders around the world during the night.

There was nothing that could not wait until later in the day.

Leo popped his organiser into his pocket, lifted his head and looked across the sunlit gardens and asked himself, yet again, why on earth he had cleared four hours from his schedule on a Monday morning to work for Cottage Orchids.

The first answer was too embarrassing to be ignored.

He had made a deal. A deal where he had actually agreed to spend hours of his valuable time in order to get his own ring back. *This was so totally pathetic that it was humiliating.*

Sara Fenchurch was a remarkable woman but

he knew that she wouldn't have put up much of a fight if he had demanded the ring then and there and kept on demanding it back until she caved under the pressure.

Except that would have made him a bully, and he had a real problem with bullies. Always had. Probably always would. And he had no plans to become one himself. Despite the level of provocation.

He had worked late into the night and over his room service breakfast finishing a report for a top client who had demanded that Leo took personal responsibility for the final recommendations—and was willing to pay to make that happen. It was a difficult case involving the hostile takeover of several chains of family-run bakeries. Bakeries that used local suppliers who could soon find themselves in trouble when the company switched to one single supplier overseas.

And even as he typed up the final recommendation he could not help thinking about Sara and her situation. Now that. Was annoying.

Helen and Caspar's friend was in trouble because of a business decision made by the one member of the Rizzi family that he respected. That did not oblige him to help her—he knew that. And yet? There was something about Sara

Fenchurch that made it impossible for him to walk away from her.

Helen or his sister would probably tell him that he was using the ring as an excuse to see her again. And even the suspicion that they could be right made his hackles rise.

She had somehow managed to squeeze under his radar and make him feel the kind of connection that he'd thought he had buried long ago.

And he had to block that out. Starting right now. Two tasks. Get in, give his advice. Ask for the inside information he needed. Then get out. *Simple.*

A few minutes later, after he had tried knocking on the door of her cottage, Leo gave up on that and headed back to the log cabin.

This time the door was slightly ajar and it looked as if Cottage Orchids might be open. He peered through the smeared and dusty window and, after a tentative knock brought no response, he turned the handle just as Sara strolled out of the nearest greenhouse with two children by her side. The boy was probably about eleven and he was clutching the hand of a little girl as he smiled at something Sara was saying.

Leo could not see what the girl looked like because her other arm was wrapped tightly around a single pot with an orchid plant in it which was so large that her head was totally obscured by the leaves. The flowers were tiny, bright orange with streamers of purple and red leaves coming out from each blossom. It was like a flower crossed with a bag of party streamers.

Sara smiled up at Leo with a tilt of her head. He noticed for the first time that, without her baseball cap, the corners of her eyes had fine white crease lines on smooth, gently tanned skin. She actually looked genuinely happy to see him.

And what made it worse was that he felt happy to see her!

Would she still be smiling if she knew how dishonest he was being? A cold, sick feeling of discomfort coiled around his gut at her misplaced trust and innocent welcoming smile.

'Good morning, Miss Fenchurch. New customers?' he asked.

'Actually, two of my best customers,' Sara replied, and then turned back to the boy. 'Now don't forget, Freddy. Tell your grandma that she only needs to water it once a week. Not once a day, like the one you gave her for Christmas.'

Freddy replied with vigorous nodding, then released his sister's hand and reached into his trouser pocket and pulled out a handful of coins.

'Oh, no. This is a replacement plant, remember? And I hope she likes it, but just bring it back if she doesn't. Now, go straight home. Bye for now. Bye.'

Leo stood next to Sara as they watched the unlikely pair stroll down the path towards the lane. The little girl had her thumb in her mouth, but wrinkled her nose at Leo and waved with her free hand before taking the boy's hand.

For one mad moment he was tempted to wrinkle his nose back at her.

'They only live in the first house down the lane,' Sara said. 'I've known the family all my life, but their grandma still doesn't know how to keep their orchids alive.'

Sara swung around on one heel. 'Good morning to you too, Mr Grainger. Ready to get to work? And, before you ask, no, I don't charge. They are my neighbours and the price list does not apply.'

She pointed in the direction of the cabin. 'I've made a start on finding the lease, but nothing so far. So I could use some help. Shall we go into the office?'

Leo replied with a tilt of his head and gestured for her to go ahead. She was wearing navy trousers today and a white blouse with little flowers embroidered on it. On any other woman it would look ridiculous and childlike and yet it somehow worked on Sara.

He enjoyed the view for a few seconds, and then stepped into the cabin behind her.

And stopped dead at the door, his brain scarcely able to take in what he was seeing.

In front of him was a scene of total disruption and what counted in his world as absolute chaos.

Two metal filing cabinets lay along one wall and on top of each were piled mountains of paperwork and folders and boxes, all bulging with sheets of paper and, as Leo walked forward, he could see most of them were invoices and receipts. More stuck out from the over-crammed drawers inside the cabinets.

The main part of the room was taken up by a long pine table—or at least he thought that it was pine, but it was difficult to make out the nature of the wood since every square inch of the surface was covered with bundles of paperwork, catalogues and unopened mail.

Peering over the top, he could see that a very ancient office chair was marooned in a sea of large sacks whose labels showed they had contained compost and fertiliser of various sorts.

That probably accounted for the very special odour in the room.

The last time he had smelt anything this bad was when the drains had been blocked for several days in his aunt's hotel and the waste disposal backed up. If Sara worked in here she must be accustomed to it, but it was making his eyes water.

'Have you been burgled?' He gagged and looked at Sara in disbelief as she rummaged around inside a large cardboard box overflowing with brown envelopes, then dropped it to the floor, revealing a very old wooden chair.

'Burgled? No,' she replied, her eyebrows squeezed together. And then she dropped her head back and shrugged. 'Oh, I see. Sorry. I suppose it has got a bit messy in here.'

He shook his head from side to side slowly in disbelief. 'This is not good, Sara. There is no way you can run an efficient business surrounded by this chaos.'

She sighed out loud and looked around as though seeing it for the first time. 'I know. There used to be a time when I knew where things were, even if they weren't filed away. But now?' Sara took a firm grip of the back of the chair. 'This is why I need help, Leo. The more I think about it, the more I realise just how much of a mess I am in. Thank goodness you turned up just in time.'

Several hours later, Sara stood next to her kitchen window and slipped Leo's ring onto her thumb, stretched out her hand and waggled it from side to side so that she could admire the sparkling diamond in all of its glory.

Helen had told her that he was single, but perhaps Leo had been married once and was widowed? Or maybe this was a treasured family heirloom only to be passed from father to son?

Whatever the reason, she had no right to keep it. Agreement or not, she should have returned it when she had the chance. But it was not too late—Leo *was* making an effort to sort through her documents and keep his side of their bargain.

Right on cue, there was a great crash and a deep groan from the direction of her log cabin office and Sara flinched with guilt. After forty minutes of frantic searching involving much grimacing and huffing and puffing, they had finally found the folder he needed on her lease, stuffed between a bundle of holiday brochures for orchid enthusiasts.

They had been in there for almost an hour when, after several attempts to work in the same room had resulted in document avalanches and an unfortunate incident with a sample of especially pungent organic fertiliser and Leo's lap, she had finally offered to make them some coffee and leave him in peace.

How had she let the paperwork and her office space deteriorate so badly?

She had planned to have a complete clean-up during the long winter months, but somehow it had never happened. Crisis had followed crisis and, before she knew it, the demand for orchids for autumn weddings had become Christmas gift specials, then Valentine's Day and then back to the spring wedding season, and now she was busier than ever.

Normally, she felt happy and warm and comforted to be in her messy place, like a little nest she had made, but she had been so ashamed to show Leo her office that morning and to see it through his eyes.

She glanced though the kitchen window towards the cabin.

Yesterday he had refused to go away and had spent a good few hours of his precious Sunday reading and learning more about the plant ranges and the most popular lines.

He had even looked interested now and again. Either that or he had been more than just polite. Perhaps he wanted to get to know her better?

Silly girl! Why should a man like Leo be interested in her? That sort of thinking would lead to even more disappointment and pain. Her mother was right—she was never going to be good enough for any man to care about her without an aristocratic name to attract them. And the sooner she accepted that fact the better.

She pushed herself upright and blinked away tears of self-pity, then quickly slipped his ring from her thumb.

There was a rustle of activity at the kitchen door and Sara quickly wrapped the ring and popped it back into her purse.

A tall slim man dressed in black was standing at her kitchen door, brushing away the dust from his clothing with his fingers. Leo!

'Oh, hello. Do you need anything? The coffee will be ready in a few minutes.'

'I need somewhere to work. I am really sorry, Sara, but that...' He opened his mouth to describe her potting shed and seemed to give up, so she stepped in for him.

'Garden office?' she suggested and was rewarded with a scowl.

'Glorified garden shed. Is driving me mad. I don't know how you can work in there,' he added and gestured towards the door. 'No filing system, no chance of finding anything. It is impossible.'

Sara checked her watch. 'You've lasted well over an hour, which is about forty minutes longer than I expected, so well done for that. Take a seat and I'll be right with you.'

Leo crossed her living room in what seemed like two strides, looked around the kitchen for somewhere to sit that was not already occupied

by piles of junk and leant against the wood-
burning stove instead. Sara frantically tried to
find a second clean mug, gave up and started
the washing-up from her hasty breakfast, before
she'd had to make the early morning deliveries
to the local florists.

The kitchen had rarely looked so messy. The
old pine dresser which ran the whole length
of the wall was loaded up with all of the bits
and pieces she would find homes for. One day.
Except that day never arrived and suddenly
every piece of junk mail, orchid catalogues, cat
toys and stray pieces of string sprang out at her.
It was a mess.

Well, at least she had cleared away the underwear from the bathroom. With a bit of luck, he
would have forgotten all about that.

'I have instant coffee or builder's tea. Any
preference?' she asked casually and was rewarded with a snort and a definite twist of one
lip from the handsome man in black who had
found a clear spot by moving one cat and several
bundles of old newspapers and was now reclin-
ing gracefully on her rickety old wooden chair
as though he was lounging on a cruise ship.

Her heart clenched. The last man who had sat
in that chair had been her ex-boyfriend, and he
had asked for a clean towel before he sat down
so that he would not dirty his suit.

She instantly sniffed away a musty smell of *goodbye and good riddance to bad rubbish,* and replaced it with the lemon balm tang of *hello, Leo Grainger.*

'What? No cappuccino machine? Ah, the delights of country living. No false airs and graces here.' And then he grinned. 'Only teasing. Tea would be great, thank you. Strong as you like. Milk, no sugar.'

She cringed inside as she caught him staring at the old pine dresser with its simple wooden shelves. Her collection of unmatched blue and white plates and bunches of keys of all shapes and sizes hanging from cup hooks screamed out in all of their unkempt glory.

If he hated the office she could hardly wait to hear his reaction to her kitchen.

'This is a lovely room,' he said without a hint of irony.

Sara dropped the teaspoon she was drying in surprise and had to start again. 'Thanks,' she replied. 'Not perhaps the neatest kitchen in the world, but it has everything I need.'

She risked a glance at him as she got the tea ready. 'You really are the most contrary person, Mr Grainger. One minute you are complaining about the state of my office and the next you are enjoying my messy kitchen. It is most confusing.'

His face wrinkled up into a wide grin and

Sara's heart gave an annoying blip in appreciation. He was handsome at the best of times but, at that moment, in his trademark immaculate black trousers and fitted shirt, he was positively the best-looking man she had ever met in her life. She had thought her ex-boyfriend handsome in an obvious, booted and city-suited slick way, but this was another level completely. The kind of charm and deep attraction that could easily lead a girl into deep waters if she did not take care. Pity that her poor tender heart did not want to take care, no matter what her head might say.

His body seemed to fill the space in the small, low ceilinged room, squeezing her into a small corner.

'Then my work is done.' He laughed and stretched his legs out even farther. 'This is your room where you relax and enjoy yourself. That—' and he pointed with one finger out of the open window towards the shed and the greenhouse only a few feet away '—is where you have to work and make a business for yourself.'

He sniffed and sat back, making the chair creak alarmingly. 'Big difference. And, as much as I appreciate your…let's say…Bohemian lifestyle, I don't think that it is helping your finances in any way.'

She passed him his tea and a plate loaded with buns and muffins. 'Please help yourself. I traded a small desk orchid for a supply of cakes first thing this morning and the village baker loved it so much she went a bit mad. And I don't have a huge freezer so...enjoy.'

'Bartering,' he whispered. 'Ah. That might explain a few things about the cash flow. That and the fact you actually give your plants away to the neighbours.'

'Do not mock,' Sara replied and sipped her tea. 'Bartering is quite a family tradition in our house, although—' and she smiled '—I suppose my grandmother did go over the top sometimes. Her accumulation of salvaged and bartered treasures was legendary. It used to drive my mum totally mad.'

Sara shuffled over to the dresser and picked up a wooden picture frame and handed it to Leo and watched in delight as his eyes widened. 'Yes, that is what it looks like. A two-woman bicycle. That's my mum on the right and grandmother on the left. Apparently, she traded a pewter teapot for a tandem bicycle so that they could cycle around the countryside in glorious splendour. She fell off the first time we tried and never rode it again. But that was her. Incorrigible.'

Leo held the photograph in silence for a few minutes, then passed it back to Sara with a quick nod. 'I never knew my maternal grandparents until a few years ago and my dad was an only child without any family to speak of. But it must have been fun living with those two ladies.'

She cocked her head and pursed her lips. 'Good times and bad. My mother hated moving back here after she got divorced. She hated the isolation and she truly hated the chaotic lifestyle my eccentric grandmother had created for herself. But she didn't have anywhere else to go and I needed a permanent home. It wasn't the best situation for either of them but it was either that or face a horrible custody battle with my dad.'

Sara smiled and cradled the mug of tea between her hands. 'And whenever the arguments got too bad, I always knew that I had somewhere calm and beautiful to escape to. The orchid houses. They were my sanctuary in the tough times and I suppose they still are now.'

She blinked away a burning in her eyes, then passed the plate back to Leo as she shuffled on her hard seat. 'Little wonder my mother has a stunning all-white modern flat in London with not one cluttered surface in sight. And that is just the way she likes it.'

Sara shook her head and shrugged at Leo, who was just finishing off his bun. 'And I have been blabbering far too long about myself. So tell me about your kitchen at home. Let me guess. Granite? Stainless steel? I want to know every detail of your designer dream.'

'Well, this is going to be fast,' he replied. 'Sorry to disappoint you, but I don't own a kitchen.'

She put down the muffin that was halfway to her lips. 'No kitchen?' she whispered in a shock.

'I don't need one,' he replied, picking up another piece of bun. 'At the moment I live in a hotel suite with full room service twenty-four hours a day. And I don't miss the washing-up one little bit.'

Leo bit into the delicious soft hot cross bun, savouring its sweet and spicy flavours. It had been so long since he had enjoyed good ordinary baked goods, although it was ironic that it should be in this cramped and crazy little kitchen, instead of the swish elegant hotels and restaurants that were part of his life of international travel.

'This is good,' he said between bites, and sipped down some of his tea. Scalding hot, just how he liked it. He was just about to take another bite when he realised that Sara had stopped talking for the first time that morning, and he looked up into her face.

What he saw there surprised and astonished him. She was looking at him—not glancing, smiling, but with a face full of sadness and pity—for him.

'What is it?' he asked. 'Is anything wrong?'

'You are living out of a hotel room,' she murmured, and her sad voice was almost breaking with emotion. Instinctively, she reached out towards him, placing a hand on top of his as though she was comforting him after some terrible grief.

Leo faltered, not knowing quite how to respond. He had a complicated relationship with the hotel trade at the best of times, but he could hardly explain that to a girl he had only just met without exposing part of himself that he did not talk to anyone about.

The fact that she had recognised something deeper in what he had said was quite remarkable. It struck him that in his daily work he met so many people but felt no connection to them.

Yet here was this girl, living in this tiny cottage, who was trying to reach out to him and comforting him for a wrong that she knew nothing about.

The silence of the moment stretched out, broken only by the birdsong on the other side of the kitchen window and the faint hiss of the kettle as it cooled.

He became aware that her short hair was not brown at all, but in the light shining through the window was actually a mixture of shades of copper and auburn and dark oak. Her eyelashes were dark brown rather than black, and her eyes—the wide eyes, which were looking at him now with such kindness and compassion, were a lighter shade of green today, flecked with golden flakes. The perfect combination against her pale golden skin flushed with pink.

She looked as lovely and as totally natural as any woman he had ever met. There was no false pretence here—this was the real thing.

And it touched him in a place in his heart, which was painful and raw and unaccustomed to being exposed to the light. And he instantly felt guilty, but he couldn't tell Sara the real reason why he was at the hotel.

'I didn't explain myself very well,' he answered, but this time in a calm voice, so as not to alarm her. 'It is only a temporary arrangement. I am actually designing my own home with my team of architects, but it's not ready yet.'

He raised his free hand and wiggled his fingers. 'Three or four months is the latest estimate. In the meantime, I am travelling a great deal to close various international projects and the hotel life fits me very well.'

'Oh, that must be so exciting.' She breathed out long and slow. 'You had me worried there for a moment.' And as he watched her a warm smile flashed across her face. 'Call me an old softie, but being without a home is one of my nightmares.' She gave a dramatic shiver for effect. 'What a horrible thought. But you probably don't know what that feels like.'

It was as if a bucket of icy water had been thrown over his head and for a moment he wanted to shout how very, very wrong she was about that.

There had been weeks and months after his parents were killed when he and his sister had been shuffled from house to house, friend to friend, until his aunt had obtained custody, stepped in and gave them a home. He had not slept, terrified that they would both be taken into care. It had been a dramatic time which he had shielded from his sister. His first act of real deception. Since then he had become a master of it.

But how could he share the pain with this girl he had only met the evening before?

He did not know how to demonstrate his compassion as openly as she had just done—he simply did not have those skills and tools in his arsenal.

So he held back. Same as usual. And flicked on his casual professional smile. It had taken him years to perfect the ability to look interested but distant at the same time.

'To answer your question,' he replied, 'I still

haven't decided between granite and one of the new glass worktops. That is still to come.'

Sliding his hand back away from Sara, and brushing away crumbs of sticky sugary baked goods from his fingers, Leo took another long sip of tea to disguise his discomfort, focused his total attention on his mug of hot tea and came up with the only thing he could think of that was relevant and would change the subject—fast.

'Right. Time to get to work, I think. I suggest we start with your financial records. Bank statements and your accounts. That should tell us exactly what the balance sheet is like and what financial options are open to you—or not.'

Sara nodded and jumped up. 'No problem. I have them all right here. All organised.'

Leo peered over the table as Sara rooted around inside the cupboards of her pine dresser, then looked on in stunned silence as she proudly presented three overstuffed, totally chaotic shoe boxes of paperwork and popped them in front of him on the table.

'There used to be sticky labels on things but I think that they must have fallen off. Hope that's not going to be too much of a problem.'

'Sara,' he asked, trying not to panic, 'don't you have these records on a spreadsheet on your computer?'

'I don't have a computer.'

His hand wiped across his mouth for a second while he tried to process that statement and failed. 'Then how do you update your website?'

'Oh, that is all in next year's plan. No computer. No website. Why? Do you think that might be a problem?'

CHAPTER SEVEN

AN HOUR and a half later, the cakes and buns were crumbs in the bottom of the cake tin and Leo was struggling to stay focused on financial reports.

Sara's kitchen was so small that he had to squeeze along one wall and stand to one side to pull out a chair so that he could sit opposite her. After the third time he kicked her in the ankle when he stretched out his legs absentmindedly, she suggested that he move around to her side of the table so that they could sit next to each other and file papers into boxes as they went.

Of course he had readily agreed. To make the paperwork easier, of course.

Nothing to do with her bruised shins at all and everything to do with the fact that he did not need an excuse to be in physical contact with Sara Fenchurch.

He had thought the log cabin office was cramped but it was positively spacious compared to her kitchen/dining room, which was jam-packed with so much clutter it should have felt claustrophobic. Instead, it felt homely and lived in.

He was close enough to see the tiny scar above the bow of her upper lip, the beauty spot just below her left ear and the fading red marks on her arm where her cat had scratched her. She smelt of shampoo, earthy compost and feminine old-money class.

What was worse, every time she stretched across to pick something up, an image of Sara wearing the lingerie he had seen on their first night kept flashing in on Leo so fast and hot that it startled him.

As though he was a mind reader, Pasha, the fluffy old sun-warmed cat, chose that moment to jump onto Leo's lap—only he didn't quite make it and dug his long claws into Leo's trousers to get a grip, piercing his skin at the same time and making him yell as Pasha scrabbled for purchase.

'Oh, no! Bad Pasha. Very bad Pasha,' Sara said and instantly broke the quiet connection as she slid her chair back and calmly picked up the cat around the middle and lifted his paws away from Leo's leg, giving Leo a quick flash down the front of her T-shirt as she bent over.

Yes. He had been right. She was wearing the

pink lace against her creamy smooth skin, and he almost groaned out loud. He was rooted to the spot, the pain in his leg forgotten.

'I am so sorry about that,' Sara said. 'We don't have many visitors and Pasha loves people. Pity the old boy can't jump so well any more. Come on, you… Outside! You have disgraced yourself!'

Sara lowered the scrabbling cat to the floor and gave him a gentle shove towards the open doors leading to the patio. Then she waggled her bottom back onto her chair and gave Leo a quick look sideways. 'You have been very quiet for much of the last hour. Should I be worried? Not that I'm complaining,' she hastened to add. 'I like quiet. Quiet suits me.'

He liked her body pressed lightly next to his side, he liked the way she bit her lower lip and hissed and groaned when she found an unopened bank statement she had dropped inside her shoe box filing system months earlier and promptly forgotten about. And he especially liked the way her hands moved when she talked, expressive, warm and completely and naturally open and unguarded. Even if her clothing was covered with cat hairs which she shed as she moved around.

She was completely different to any of the women whom he met in his life. And it totally disarmed him. All of the defence mechanisms he had built up, and the surface gloss and prestigious trappings of success did not mean one thing here. He found it bizarrely calm and reassuring that there were people like Sara Fenchurch still around. Shame that it also made his job, and his task at that moment, particularly difficult.

Focus. That was it. Back to the work at hand.

'Your finances are not looking good, Sara,' he replied in a soft voice and half turned in his hard seat so that he could face her.

'I think I liked quiet better, but yes, I know, and that's with three greenhouses. If I lose two of them?' She sighed and blew out long and slow. 'Any ideas you have would be very welcome now. Please.'

Leo looked into her wide concerned eyes in silence for a few seconds, his brow creased with concentration.

'There are a couple of less pleasant options involving finding a day job which are fairly obvious but I suggest we keep those as last resorts. Does that shudder mean yes? Good.'

Leo picked up one of the bundles of receipts.

'You don't have a website and, from what I can see on paper, you don't spend any money on telling people how wonderful your orchids are and where they can find you. Your main cus-

tomers are local florists and garden centres plus
a few hotels and restaurants, but all within about
a twenty-mile radius of where we are sitting. Is
that a reasonable assessment?'

Sara sat back and grinned, then tapped two
fingers against her forehead in a quick salute.
'You got all that just from a few scraps of paper?
I am impressed. And yes, you're right. All of my
customers came by word of mouth really. One
person tells another and I get a call.'

She started to bite her thumbnail, and then
pushed her hands onto her lap.

'Marketing and promotion were on that list
with the computer and the website. Looks like I
have left it too late. Doesn't it?'

'Not necessarily,' Leo replied and leant forward just a little, his elbow resting on the table.
'What I am looking for is some way to make
your orchid nursery stand out from all of the
other plant nurseries in this area. Once you find
that unique aspect, then you can start to create
a whole new brand for yourself and really get
started on the marketing. That is when you need
your computer and your website. With a new
name and a new professional image you can
begin to charge higher prices for your plants.'

He slid back and gestured towards the kitchen
window. 'More orders, more income, more land
you can rent. How does that sound? Sara? You're

shaking your head. I thought you wanted to hear some realistic suggestions.'

'I do. I really do, but frankly the whole branding thing scares me silly. It is exactly what I wanted to get away from when I left my job in London. And I don't want to change the name of my company. I like calling myself Cottage Orchids. It says a lot about me. That has to stay.'

'And where is this cottage? And what makes it special? I don't even have any hint where the plants are grown from that name or who is growing them. For all I know, your cottage could be a huge corrugated iron warehouse in central London.'

Sara gasped in horror and threw a paperclip at him which bounced off his chest. 'That is a horrible thing to say. What do you want me to call it? *Phalaenopsis-R-Us?* Or perhaps we should go for something like my grandmother's cunning idea? Just wait until you see this.'

There was a great shuffling of chairs and table but Sara was able to squeeze out, slide along to her dresser and, after a few seconds of a spectacular view of the back of her trousers and much pulling and pushing, she emerged with a piece of once white card with a title written in very flowery and curving script which Sara passed to Leo as she read it out from memory in the highest, whiniest, poshest voice Leo had ever heard. And he had heard plenty in his time, but this girl had it down perfectly.

'*Lady Fenchurch's Kingsmede Manor Heritage Orchids.*'

She sighed and went to refill the kettle. 'Can you imagine it? I would have coachloads of tourists turning up in the lane expecting to find a huge museum dedicated to my orchid hunting ancestors, a team of professional scientists cloning endangered orchid specimens in a sterile lab and several acres of tropical glasshouses. There should probably be a gourmet café and gift shop on the side with photos of my grandmother wearing her tiara.'

A snort was followed by a hollow laugh. 'I could charge admission! Until they actually realise that all I have left is one orchid house and this cottage to show for three generations of orchid-mad ancestors and they all demand their money back. I might have got away with it when I was living in the Manor, but in a few weeks…? No, Leo. The last thing I want is to pretend to be something I am not. Kingsmede Manor Heritage Orchids should be grown at Kingsmede Manor. End of story. And would you prefer coffee or tea?'

'Tea, please. And I love it.'

'Love what?' Sara replied, looking around the room until she realised that he was grinning and practically drooling at the piece of card she had just passed him.

The penny dropped. And so did her chin.

'Oh, you cannot be serious. Please, no. Not that. There has to be something else we can do, Leo,' Sara said. 'Think. There are three generations of my family who have worked to create these orchids. I might not be an orchid-hunter like they were, but I have to do something to carry on the tradition they started. If I don't, then everything they did would be lost, and I can't bear the thought of that happening.'

'Then try and see this name with new eyes. *It is inspired.* I'm serious. Don't you see it?'

Leo grabbed the card, his eyes shining with excitement as though he had just unearthed some ancient treasure from a muddy field. 'You need a brand that launches you head and shoulders above the competition—and it's right here, staring you in the face. All you have to do is combine your name with your family heritage in growing orchids. It would make all the difference.'

He grinned, trying to contain his enthusiasm. 'Why on earth didn't you tell me that you had a title? Any links to the nobility are a terrific selling feature. Believe me. You will not come up with anything better than this.'

One of her hands pressed hard onto the table-

top, palm down for support, while the teaspoon
she was holding in the other hand waved widely
in the air, splattering droplets of cold tea across
the paperwork.

'A selling feature. Oh, that is just perfect.
The entire history of my mother's family comes
down to how I can use my heritage as a *terrific
selling feature*. How foolish of me not to think
of that before.'

Her hand stilled and Leo could see the faint
tremble in her fingers but, when she spoke,
Sara's voice was intense, quiet and absolutely
crystal-clear and resolute.

'I need to make something very clear. I don't
have a title and I never have had a title. My
grandmother was the daughter of an Earl but
she left that world behind when she married a
commoner. Sorry, Leo. She may have kept her
courtesy title but any links to the peerage ended
right there. If I have learnt anything in my life
it is that having a title is a curse, not a bless-
ing. That's why I won't do it. I won't lie. And I
certainly will not use my grandmother's title to
sell my orchids.'

And just like that Leo's heart contracted and he
felt a powerful cord pulling him towards Sara
from a place deep inside that he had forgotten
was even there.

It was so sudden and so powerful that he almost moved backwards to counteract the strength of the invisible bond that was locking him into this girl. But the tension was so strong there was no way that he could break it by the force of his will.

This was no trivial frisson of physical attraction. This was something else. Something much, much bigger which bypassed his head and hit him hard in the heart and the gut. Fast and hard and brutal in its intensity, but so miraculously uplifting his heart soared.

And the feeling knocked him sideways and speechless.

Here was this girl he had only just met, opening her heart and spilling out her feelings and her loyalties onto this messy table, while he just sat there, his secrets buried so deep inside his chest for so many years that he had almost convinced himself that they no longer existed. Until moments like this one when he saw how his life could have been so very different if he had taken a different path all those years ago. A path where he did not have to deceive the world around him every day of his working life just as he deceived himself to get through the day.

He had kept his secrets and resentments and pain to himself for so long that they had become almost like a story rather than the truth. It made it easier that way.

Until someone like Sara came along and in a few minutes told him that his story was not unique. Far from it.

Sara's grandmother had sacrificed her inheritance for love, just as his mother had left her wealthy family behind to be with her soulmate. And the aftermath of those earthquake decisions were still rippling through the lives of their descendents.

They were so alike it terrified him.

He had not told Sara one word about his own past and yet he felt as though she knew him and what was going on inside his head even better than his own sister. His aunt saw driving ambition and the search for status and position. But Sara? Sara had the power to disarm him with a few simple words as she wrapped her small fingers around his heart and squeezed.

And the walls around his heart started to feel just a little less solid, as though tiny cracks had appeared and alarm bells were ringing, warning him to be careful.

There was still time to repair the damage and rebuild this flash outer mask the world saw when they looked at Leo Grainger.

He should walk away from this connection and from Sara, wish her well for the future and simply get on with his life. He could deny the attraction. Why not? He had given her an option for a business idea and kept his side of the bargain.

He could leave any time he wanted. Just get up and go back to the hotel and drive away.

Leaving her to lose everything she had worked for.

He looked up to see Sara trying to make tea, only as he watched this pretty girl, her hands were so jittery the teaspoon fell onto the flagstones and she was so overcome that it was all she could do to cling onto the worktop.

Instinctively and without conscious thought for the consequences, Leo squeezed out of his chair and crossed the few feet that separated them and pressed his chest against the back of her T-shirt, wrapping his arms around her waist and enclosing her in his embrace.

He wanted to kiss away her fears and pain so badly that he could already imagine what she would taste like from the perfume of her shampoo in her hair and the aroma of coffee and baking. Honest smells. Real. Homely. All Sara.

But that would be too much too soon—for both of them.

Instead he pressed his chin onto her shoulder in silence and pulled her a little tighter towards him in the circle of his arms, savouring the feeling of her warm cheek against the side of his face, waiting for her to say something—anything—but not wanting to break this bond which connected them by something as powerful as words.

Her chest rose and fell several times before he sensed the tension ease away from her shoulders. His reward came as she relaxed back just a fraction of an inch farther into his arms, as though she was willing him to take her weight.

And his heart sang. For one precious moment he allowed a tiny, small and oh, so precious bubble of something other people would call happiness to burst into existence and he sucked in a breath of shock and surprise and delight.

Sara instantly stiffened and clasped onto his hands, drawing them away from her waist so they could rest lightly on her hips.

Leo stepped back just far enough to allow some space between them so that she could turn and face him.

The palms of her hands pressed gently onto the front of his shirt and her heartbeat increased and was so loud he could almost hear it. Every instinct in his body was screaming that this was right, but she had still not raised her head.

She wasn't ready for that. Not yet. His hand lifted so that he could caress the back of her head, making him tremble at the intensity of the waves of delicious sensation at the ends of his fingers.

His voice was low and so close to her ear that it was more of a whisper. 'I understand why you don't want to use her name,' he said. 'Better than you can imagine.'

'How can you possibly understand?' she answered, her words muffled into his chest. 'You are part of the Rizzi family. You have everything you could possibly want in life.'

His hand slid down her back from her hairline and he could almost feel the mental and physical barriers coming down between them as he pulled back and lifted her chin so that he could look at her.

And what he saw in those green-and-gold eyes made the breath catch in his throat. The intensity. The confusion. The regret. It was all there.

The only thing this woman deserved was the truth.

'I understand you because my mother gave up a life of luxury and privilege to be with the man she loved. Her own family disowned her for choosing my father over them, but she did not regret it for one minute. That's why I understand why you admire your grandmother so very much.'

Leo's fingers caressed the back of her head

as she gasped in astonishment, her eyes locked onto his.

'And that is why I am going to help you honour her memory in any way I can,' he said, smiling.

'What do you mean?' she breathed, her eyes wide and her skin flushed. 'Honour her memory?'

'From what you've told me, your orchid houses are a living memory to everything she created here and the deep love she felt for this place. And that is too special to let go. Am I right?'

'Yes, of course. They are her orchids! I am simply carrying on the work she started and trying to repay all of the love she gave me over the years at the same time. And yes, she did love this place. And so do I.'

Leo slowly and gently slid his hands down her arms in wide slow circles, and watched her sigh of pleasure as he did so.

'Then we had better get back to work. Although I do have one more question before we get started. How do you hunt orchids?'

'You hunt them in the wild, of course,' she replied with a laugh and started waving her arms around. 'The craze for orchids started in the early eighteen-hundreds and reached its peak with the Victorians and Edwardians. Everyone

simply had to have exotic orchids in their greenhouses to keep up with the fashion—it was a
mad and exciting time. Explorers were sent all
over the world to collect hundreds of species
of orchids of every possible size and shape and
colour and it was dangerous work.'

Sara paused for a second and pointed to a
sepia print on the wall of a fine-looking man
with a handlebar moustache who was standing
with his arms folded and wearing a stiff-looking
tweed suit. 'Alfred Fenchurch almost died of
yellow fever and got caught up in a revolution,
but on top of that there were all kinds of other
tropical diseases, wild animals, fierce tribes and
natural disasters. Travelling in Central America
or Papua New Guinea at the turn of the century
was no joke.'

She slipped away from him just enough to
turn the kettle on and Leo mourned the loss
of that deep connection that he had not even
realised was there until she moved out of the
comfort of his arms.

'The Fenchurch family caught orchid fever
and it has been in the blood ever since. Would
you like to see some photographs of the house
in its heyday?'

Sara swept past him and practically skipped
across the small room, energised and excited,
and more animated than Leo had seen her since

the party. He could only look on in wonder as she rummaged around at the bottom of the dresser and pulled out a large hat box wrapped with string.

In an instant she had swept her bundles of finance papers to one side to create a space on the table with a lot more enthusiasm than she had for doing filing and admin, and Leo watched in amazement as the hat box sprang open like a children's toy and bundles of photographs and documents tied with ribbon and, in some cases, garden twine, cascaded out across the desk.

All he could do was sigh and shake his head. These old sepia prints, faded in places and torn in others, were obviously of great historical value—and here they were, all stuffed in a flimsy hat box with broken sides in a draughty kitchen which was filled with steam one minute and heat from the oven the next.

Did Sara not realise how very precious these family memories were?

His own mother had brought very few photographs of her Rizzi family with her when she had eloped to marry his father in secret, and he had no true sense of the heritage she had left behind apart from the stories and newspaper clippings she'd kept in an album at the bottom of her wardrobe.

He would have loved this kind of treasure

trove to delve into and explore his past as a boy, but that was impossible. His aunt had answered many of his questions following his parents' death, but it was not the same as sitting on a bed with his mother as she pointed to the faces of her family in newspapers and magazines.

Perhaps that was why he simply grinned and dived into the box so that he could share Sara's simple joy and excitement and enthusiasm at the mere sight of these photographs. She passed him image after image, explaining who each person was and what they were doing in their tropical costumes and exotic settings. But, just as she passed him a photograph of her great-great-grandfather, he noticed a folded piece of chart paper tucked down the side of the hat box.

'Is that a map of their adventures?' he asked.

'Oh, no,' Sara replied and drew out the page and quickly unfolded it. 'This was one of the original designs of the tropical glasshouses. That was when there was real money in the family—' she laughed '—and they could afford to hire one of the most famous garden designers in Britain to create something very special to house the orchids. Back then, there were hundreds of plants from all over the world with a full-time staff to look after them.'

'May I?' he asked. 'I've always loved architectural designs.'

Beautiful calligraphy ran down the side of the page and Leo smiled in delight at the stunning pristine craftsmanship of the hand drawn plans dated over a hundred years ago. They were some of the most beautiful architectural designs he had ever seen, and he instantly recognised the name of the designer.

'This is amazing,' he whispered breathlessly, aware that Sara was sitting so close to him that the side of her body was pressed tight against his as they looked at the chart together. 'Were these glasshouses ever made?'

'The money ran out,' she said with a tut. 'The two Victorian glasshouses I use for my orchids were based on a smaller version of the plan, but of course this was only one part of a much greater design. The other evening on the terrace I was telling you about the wonderful gardens that used to be here when my grandmother was a girl. The orangery and main conservatory were still in place then and they must have been quite magnificent.'

'What happened to them? Were they damaged or destroyed?'

'My great-grandmother sold them after the war when times were hard. She was a widow on her own and she couldn't afford the staff to run them. There are a few photographs in the stack here if you'd like to look at them.'

Leo watched in delight as Sara drew out photographs, then more photographs of her family and their servants standing in front of beautiful ornate glass structures next to the house he knew as Kingsmede Manor Hotel. And, as she did so, the first glimmer of an idea flitted through his mind. An idea for something so remarkable and grand that it startled him by the sheer exuberant ambition of it.

What if he could convince his aunt to invest in restoring the gardens?

He had been looking for something unique which would distinguish this hotel from all the other country hotels in the area—something which would attract new guests with different interests. Perhaps Sara Fenchurch had just given him something to work on? And it could just save her business at the same time.

It was incredibly frustrating that he could not share his ideas with her without giving away his aunt's secret but he would not raise her hopes until he had something more tangible. Then he would tell her everything. But in the meantime he needed to gather together all of the information she had.

Drat. There went another one of those bubbles of happiness again. This was starting to become habit-forming and it only happened when he was around Sara. Strange, that.

'Sara, this design is fantastic. I would love to see everything you have on the original plans for the garden design and glasshouses of the Manor. Will you help me?'

CHAPTER EIGHT

NORMALLY, at six-thirty on a Tuesday morning, Leo was in the gym of the stunning London hotel which he had chosen to make his home. It was convenient, warm and he could sneak back to his room in the private elevator, knowing that a delicious breakfast would be served at his convenience.

Kingsmede Manor had proved deficient on both counts. No gym and no room service at that time in the morning unless he wanted a stale roll and coffee.

There were compensations, of course. Starting with the fact that he was alone on a sunny morning and was about to spend some of the day with one of the most intriguing and remarkable people he had met for a long time, and who was probably stamping her foot at that very moment and wondering where on earth he had got to.

Sara had promised to show him some of the local area from the passenger seat of her deliv-

ery van while he took her through a few ideas
for the business.

She would be driving.

He could hardly wait.

He shoved his hands deep into his trouser
pockets and marched down the patio steps and
in minutes was across the lane and just about to
knock on her front door when there was a rat-
tat of a car horn with a musical chime, and he
turned and stared in disbelief at the remarkable
example of decrepitude in automotive engineer-
ing which was rolling down the lane towards
him.

The tiny delivery van had originally been
white, but was now more of a dirty, rusty pale
yellow, decorated with pictures of orchids of
various colours and sizes which were scattered
around the words 'Cottage Orchids'. It was so
girly and unprofessional he could hardly believe
it.

Wait a minute! Cottage Orchids! Oh, no—it
couldn't be! But there could be no mistake. His
eyes closed for a second when he realised the
true horror of the situation he had got himself
into.

Sure enough, the engine juddered to a halt,
the driver's door clanked open and Sara stepped
out and he did a double take.

She was wearing a smart outfit of navy trousers and navy T-shirt with 'Cottage Orchids' embroidered in gold letters on the shoulder. Her hair was swept back with a navy bandanna and she looked cute, attractive, gobsmacking lovely, and parts of his body did a little happy dance.

Pop music blared out from the radio, bright and cheerful, and in total contrast to the look on her face.

Sara stood back and crossed her arms, her feet squarely on the ground in a stance that screamed out that she was not best pleased.

'You are so late. It is not funny,' she said. 'I was going to give you three more minutes before heading off on my own. You do know I have five deliveries to make this morning? Which, as you pointed out yesterday, are actually quite important to my income.'

Leo looked deep into her eyes and replied in a serious voice, 'I like the outfit. Very classy. Now, about the delivery van…'

She shrugged, uncrossed her arms and patted the roof of the once white vehicle, her mood instantly transformed to one of pleasure. 'You noticed. I know—' she grinned and wrinkled her nose in pleasure '—isn't she fantastic? I had to paint the letters myself, of course, to get it just right, but Mitzi has never let me down once. She knows I love her.'

'Mitzi?'

'Mitzi my microvan, of course. She's electric and quiet. Not the fastest little motor in the world but that's okay. And she's so cheap to run. This is a good thing.'

Leo decided that it would be dangerous to his health to mock Mitzi or offend her owner.

'If you give me directions to the first stop, I'll follow in my own car—that will leave more room for you and your plants inside...' And coughed twice before adding, 'The lovely Mitzi.'

Sara's eyes narrowed, and she gave him a hard look for a few moments, then she threw out her arms to both sides and laughed until she had to bend over and grasp hold of her knees to recover.

'Oh, I should have guessed it.' She laughed and wiped away tears from her eyes. 'Leo Grainger, you are a car snob. A full on, totally over the top car snob. I bet that you even have those cute little driving gloves so you don't get nasty sweat on your steering wheel. Am I right?'

'They were a Christmas present from my sister,' he replied indignantly with a twist of his lip. 'And I am not a car snob. I merely appreciate, let's say, the finer things in life. And poor old Mitzi here has seen better days. I do have some standards.'

Her reply was a gentle smile, followed by a short nod. Then she reached into the van, took out the keys and tossed them to him.

He caught the keys one-handed as if he had been waiting for them.

And they stood there, smiling at one another like a pair of idiots in the morning sunshine.

Three hours later, Leo collapsed down into Mitzi's driver's seat outside a very pretty florist shop in a village ten miles away from Kingsmede, turned on the engine and banged his head twice against the steering wheel, his arms hanging loosely on either side of his body as he waited for his blood pressure to reduce until he was calm enough to drive.

'Oh, it wasn't that bad,' said Sara, pulling off her gardening gloves. 'They loved you in the shop.'

'She offered me a job selling cut flowers!'

'I know! And the manager is usually so shy!' Sara paused and sniffed. 'But well done. You will be pleased to know that this was our very last stop so you can turn off the charm offensive and speed all the way back to the Manor.'

'Twenty miles an hour,' Leo sobbed dramatically. 'Our top speed has been twenty miles an hour! I feel so ashamed. Is there a taxi rank in this village?'

'Hey!' she replied and hit him on the arm with her delivery notes. 'The bus goes once a week so you are stuck with me or hitching a lift. But, as a special treat, I will let you sit in the passenger seat going home.' Then she flung open her door and was about to jump out of the van, when she surprised him by closing the door quickly and shuffling down in her seat.

'Try to look interested in this paperwork,' she hissed, and passed him a bundle of loose papers from the floor of the van before reaching under his seat for a green baseball cap, which she pulled down hard over her head.

'Er, Sara... What is going on, and why should I pretend to be interested in your order sheets?'

'Shush,' she hissed out of the corner of her mouth. 'Do you see the lady who is coming out of the grocers? Beige suit. Cream handbag.'

Leo glanced casually through the windscreen before nodding and staring intently at an invoice with a muddy shoeprint on it. 'Blonde, mid-fifties, make-up from the same era. Do you owe her money?'

'Much worse,' Sara hissed, bending across to stare at the papers. 'She has been trying to set me up with her son for the past eighteen months and the woman will not take no for an answer. For some bizarre reason she is convinced that her son will rocket up the promotion ladder if he has a lady with a classy family name on his arm. And at the moment I'm his best bet for a trophy girlfriend.'

Sara had barely got the words out of her mouth when there was a small tap on the passenger window and Leo waved gently at the lady that Sara was trying to avoid, who was giving him a filthy look through the glass.

Sara instantly rolled down the window and smiled politely. 'Good afternoon, Mrs Tadley. Isn't it a lovely day?'

'Oh, indeed,' she replied, staring intently at Leo as she spoke. 'How nice to see you, Lady Sara. I was hoping to catch up with you about our summer soirée. I do hope you can join us.' And then she looked over towards Leo and smiled through clenched teeth. 'And perhaps your new friend would like to join us?'

'Oh, my business adviser is only in town for a few days, Mrs Tadley,' Sara replied casually. 'And we are on a very tight schedule.'

'Business adviser? Oh, yes, how clever of you,' she replied, clearly relieved that Leo was not a love interest. Then she lowered her voice and stuck her head into the van. 'I have heard about your problems with the hotel, Lady Sara. It must be terribly distressing. Do call me if there is anything my family can do to help.'

From where he was sitting, Leo could see

Sara's fingers were clutched so tightly around the paperwork that her knuckles were turning white with the strain of the self-restraint.

'That is very kind of you, Mrs Tadley. Thank you. I will. Have a good afternoon.' And she gave a small finger wave and smiled sweetly as the window slid up, ending the conversation.

Leo blinked. Proud, stubborn and independent. With very good manners. This was a very different side to the girl he had met at the buffet table in the hotel on Saturday night and danced with under the moonlight.

And she totally took his breath away.

His admiration clicked to a higher level.

'Well, that was interesting,' he said, 'Lady Sara.'

'Actually—' she blinked '—my mother named me Eloise Sara Jane Marchant Fenchurch de Lambert but, seeing as you are my business adviser, Sara will do splendidly, my dear Leonardo.' And she twirled her hand in the air as though giving him a regal wave.

'Delighted to meet you, Eloise. And I don't believe that we have been formally introduced. Leonardo Reginald Costantino Rizzi Grainger at your service, madam.' And he bowed towards her with as much grace as the cramped cab would allow.

'Leonardo Reginald. Oh, my.' Sara clapped

her hand over her mouth and pressed her lips together before she embarrassed herself.

'Parents do have a lot to answer for.' He shrugged and looked nonchalantly out of the window at the small street.

'That they do,' she croaked out, 'Reggie.'

'At last! Something we can both agree on, Eloise.' And he returned her smile, lifting into the cutest dimple on the right side of his mouth.

It was not the smile of a slick city power broker but much more like a naughty boy who had been caught enjoying himself far too much.

'Eloise and Reggie's Floral Specialities. That does have a certain ring to it, doesn't it? Any chance you could be available a couple of mornings a week? I could pay you in orchids and bartered cakes. I predict a great future. What do you say?'

Leo found something fascinating on the roof of the cab and tapped one finger against his chin as though he was giving her proposal serious thought, then shook his head. 'I don't think that *particular* brand would do much to sell orchids. But thank you for the invitation. If I decide to change direction, I shall give you a call.'

'It's a deal, and you could be right,' Sara continued with a chuckle, checking in her door mirror that she was now safe. 'They all know perfectly well that I am not a Lady anything and never will be, but as far as the residents of Kingsmede are concerned I am my grandmother's heir and the rules of peerage do not apply. Not much good having a trophy girlfriend if you can't brag, is there?'

She shrugged and laughed out loud. 'It's a good thing I've given up on the dating scene, that's for sure. No more boyfriends for me. I can't tell you what a relief that is.'

'No more boyfriends?' Leo laughed dismissively. 'You can't mean that. I take it that the Kingsmede singles scene is a tad limited if Mrs Tadley is anything to go by. And yes, I am driving us home. I can't take any more excitement this early in the day.'

Sara stared at him down her nose as Mitzi pulled away from the kerb, and then snorted, 'And what makes you think that I don't have a fascinating social life? It might not be up to London standards, but Pasha and I have a splendid time and there is always the occasional costume party at the hotel.'

She sat up a little straighter in the passenger seat as Leo coughed disbelievingly and waved at a couple of pedestrians. 'Do not mock. I am actually thinking of taking a short working holiday next spring. There are quite a few companies running holidays for orchid enthusiasts who need specialist guides and it would be brilliant to see what other folks are doing.'

She glanced over in his direction. Leo had his lips pressed firmly together and was staring hard at the road immediately in front of him.

'Now, don't look like that. These tours are very popular.'

He responded by tapping the steering wheel. 'Oh, I don't doubt it,' he said in a low voice. 'In fact, would you mind if I borrowed a few of your holiday brochures when we get back?'

Sara's mouth fell open with a thud, then closed again. 'You want to go on holiday with a team of orchid-mad gardeners touring glass-houses? I would like to see that.'

'Research. And here's another idea. Seeing as the local social scene is a little limited, I was wondering if I could persuade you to join me for dinner in the hotel this evening as my guest? Say about seven? You've been kind enough to feed me baked goods on a regular basis so please allow me to return the favour. What do you say? Are you willing to risk the hotel cooking again? There would be just the two of us this time.'

'Dinner?' she replied in a low voice and stared out of the van window at the other cars, the fields—anywhere, in fact, that did not require her to look towards Leo.

'You may have heard of it. Meal. Usually taken in the evening involving hot food which is cooked by someone else. Can be fun. I have tried it myself many times and would heartily recommend it.'

Sara took a tighter hold on the paperwork and unfolded it as a distraction for her hands while her poor brain tried to process the fact that Leo Grainger had just asked her out to dinner. At the hotel. Just the two of them.

Somewhere in the back of her brain a choir was singing hallelujahs, blowing trumpets and holding up banners that read *Sara has a date with Leo, Sara has a date with Leo!* while the quieter contingent was sitting with their arms folded and shaking their heads.

She stole a glance sideways while he was distracted by a roundabout where the Kingsmede version of the rush hour was in full swing. Pension day.

Leo gorgeous-from-the-shoes-up Grainger had asked her out for a meal. Not a date. He had never mentioned that, far from it. But it was a meal and she would be his guest. In a hotel restaurant.

That sounded like a date, smelled like a date and she could almost taste the delicious totally unaffordable food that the hotel had become famous for. If she went as his date.

Most girls would jump at the chance to be in the same room as Leo, never mind be his dinner companion. She would be the envy of every other woman in the room.

But she was not like other girls. And she had already been down this road before one too many times.

It was ironic in some ways. She had just accused Mrs Tadley of seeing her as a trophy piece of arm candy—when that was exactly what she would be doing with Leo and what she had done with every other handsome and stylish man who had ever asked her out. She was the one who used to like trophy boyfriends.

She had used them and they had used her.

Weird that she had never realised that until this very moment.

She looked down at the creased and now totally screwed up receipts and her eyes slid over to the driver's seat. The crease was still crisp in Leo's black trousers, which were made of fabric so fine and soft she longed to touch it and stroke his leg.

Of course she wanted to spend the evening with Leo.

Of course she wanted to hear him laugh and find out how he ate his peas and what kind of food he liked best in the world.

Of course she wanted to have her heart broken

yet again when he left her behind to go back
to his high-flying life in London. He would
be the trophy date to end all trophy dates, and
would probably ruin her for anyone else for a
long time. And then she would have to face him
again at Helen and Caspar's wedding. *Oh, no.*

*Going out to dinner with Leo would be so
wonderful that it would be terrible.*

Smoothing out the pages of her now crushed
receipts with the palms of her hands in the vain
hope of making them legible, Sara lifted her
head and looked from side to side.

'Thanks for the invite but I'm already booked
for dinner this evening. I would really love some
of those fondant chocolates if they are on the
menu, though. Would you mind leaving some
at reception for me?'

'You're turning me down?' He gave her a
confused glance before focusing on his driving.
'Should I change my cologne? I don't usually
have this much trouble persuading ladies to dine
with me.'

She smiled longingly at him. 'No, and please
don't change a thing.'

'I refuse to be thwarted. Let's pretend that we
are having our dinner conversation right now.
Driving along in this van.'

'Pretend we are having dinner together? I

wish you'd warned me. I would have changed into something a little less…well…navy.'

He raised his right hand for a second. 'You look enchanting. In fact I have not been able to take my eyes off you since you entered the room. Could I interest you in some chilled pink champagne while we look at the menu?'

'Oh, yes, please.' She wriggled, suddenly feeling much better, safe in the familiar comfort of Mitzi. 'French, of course.'

'Absolutely. So, while we are waiting for the starters to arrive, I'll make small talk about city life. You mentioned that you used to work in London, but I have no idea how you spent your time. What did you do? Where did you eat? I'm curious. Perhaps we know the same restaurants?'

'Ah, yes, my old city life. My mother still lives there, you know. Do you know Pimlico at all? Very chic. As for my job, I worked as a general dogsbody for my mother's friends who ran a company renting out luxury villas. They paid me very little to sort out the problems their guests were having all over the world. When I was in London I usually ate out with my former boyfriend who was far more interested in my family connections than in me. He had nice manners, nice clothes and my mother totally approved of him.'

'Ouch. To both. Please have another glass of virtual champagne.'

'Don't mind if I do. Thanks. Most delicious.'

Leo stopped the car and waved some pedestrians across the road before moving on. 'Do you get up to London much to see your mother?'

'Ah, that would be no. We had a major steaming argument three years ago and as a result I gave up my job in London to open an orchid nursery in rural Hampshire and she has never been back. We haven't spoken much since.'

'Three years! I find it hard to believe that you're still not talking after three years!' Leo said in a shocked voice. 'You have to be one of the easiest people to talk to that I have ever met. What happened?'

Sara looked at him in silence. And suddenly the good opinion of this man mattered a lot more to her than she would have thought possible. She simply could not face the idea that he thought badly of her. It had been so long since she had told anyone or even thought about those sad days that it would be a relief to explain her decision to someone who did not know her history.

'Do you really want to know? Then watch out. Here comes the main course. Roast beef. All dried up. Overcooked. Tough and stringy.'

Her hands busied themselves pulling at a

loose thread in her peaked cap while she deliberately tried to avoid making eye contact with Leo. 'My grandmother had not been well for some time, but she insisted on living on her own at the Manor and we used to visit at weekends and make a fuss of her. Well, the crunch came when my grandmother had to go into hospital and needed someone to take care of her when she came out.'

Sara lifted up the cap and pointed it at the windscreen. 'The villa company owed me about four weeks' holiday but every time I asked for it there was always some crisis which needed my urgent attention or their world would stop. I finally pleaded for one week just to be here with my grandmother.'

She dropped the hat and fell back against her seat. 'Of course that didn't last very long. Three days into my holiday I had a pleading phone call telling me that there was an emergency in the Caribbean and I was the only person in the world who could sort it out. I refused to go so they called my mother, who told me quite clearly that I could not let her friends down, so she offered to take my place with my grandmother until I got back. And I was foolish enough to believe that she would actually do it.'

Sara closed her eyes and shook her head slowly from side to side. 'I should have known better.' She looked over at Leo. 'Do you know what the emergency was? The jacuzzi at the villa was not hot enough for the guests. And nobody else was capable of adjusting the temperature. I called the plumber. I watched the plumber adjust the temperature control. Then I came home. And what did I find? My grandmother, alone, cold and hungry. My mother had lasted a total of two days before driving back to London after falling out over some trivial thing.'

Sara started tugging at the hat in her lap. 'I will not repeat what I said to my mother because it was not very dignified or polite, but let's just say that she was totally shocked that a girl with my expensive education had such an extensive vocabulary of expletives, including some she had never heard before.'

There was a pause as she realised that she had just pulled the visor off her hat by tugging at it too fiercely. 'It was the biggest row we've ever had. And at the end of it I was so furious that I told her that I had no intention of working for a pittance for one day longer while her friends lived in Switzerland in the lap of luxury. If she wanted to help them then she could do the work herself. She told me that I had always been an ungrateful child who would end up alone and unloved. I resigned over the telephone ten minutes later and I have never looked back. Not once. I don't miss the travel and I don't miss the problems.'

'But you miss your mother,' he said in a low voice. And in the relative silence of their small enclosed space his words seemed to echo into her brain and reverberate there for a second.

One side of her face twitched into a half smile. 'Sometimes. She certainly taught me that not every mother loves her own child all of the time. I just didn't know that it showed.'

'What happened to the boyfriend? The one who was only interested in your grandmother's title. Did he offer to come and help?'

Sara laughed and rolled her eyes. 'Oh, yes,' she replied. 'He turned up for my grandmother's funeral, then took one look at my cottage, compared it to Kingsmede Manor and decided that my new life in the country was not one he would enjoy. But he was very generous—he did offer to wait for me to come to my senses and come back to London. Two weeks later he ran off to Australia with the office junior he had taken to a conference and sent me a text accusing me of not giving enough priority to our relationship.'

Her shoulders shook off the memory with a dramatic shudder. 'Last time I heard, he was happily dating the daughter of a Scottish earl. And good luck to him and very good luck to her because she's going to need it. And I rather think that I have eaten far too much of the tough meaty part of the meal and not left any for you. Your turn.'

'My turn?'

'Oh, yes. I may be your guest at this splendid feast but I should be polite and try and learn more about my dining companion. Especially now that he knows all about my fierce bad temper and unforgiving nature.'

'True. And under the circumstances it would be rude not to offer you some business advice. Although, after what you have just said about your bad temper, I suspect that my suggestion might not go down very well. Perhaps I should wait until you have eaten your dessert first to sweeten you up.'

Sara sucked in a breath and looked at him for a second. 'I don't like the sound of that,' she said, 'but okay. I did ask you to help me. Go ahead. Bring on the gateau but let me prepare myself first.'

She gritted her teeth and clutched onto the dashboard with both of her hands. 'Okay,' she said, 'I'm ready. Hit me with it. You have my full attention.'

'Don't look so scared! This is just one idea. I was on the phone to a venture capitalist friend of mine yesterday who is interested in unusual start-up companies—like yours!'

She practically leapt out of her seat but Leo gestured with the flat of his hand for her to sit back down again.

'Before you get excited, he will want to know that you can guarantee constant supply of top quality plants to the marketplace. Right now, I can only see one way to make sure that happens. You need to move the two old orchid houses.'

Sara felt as though all of the air had been sucked out of the van, making her head spin, but she could not—dare not—move until she'd heard what Leo had to say.

Leo paused while he turned back onto the main road where the traffic was much heavier. 'I have been looking at land prices around Kingsmede and they are higher than I expected but, with the right business plan and a new marketing campaign, you could afford to rent the extra space you need on the other side of the village. Shall I give him a call? And now you have gone quiet. Tell me what you're thinking. Interested?'

Sara stared at Leo wide-eyed, scarcely believing what he had just said. They had been working together in the same kitchen and he had not understood one single thing about why she was there and why she had stayed in this cottage in Kingsmede when she could have moved anywhere in the world. And how could he? When she had not bothered to explain it to him. She sighed at her own stupidity.

Why should he understand when even her own mother did not understand fully?

'Take down my grandmother's orchid houses?' she replied. 'Have you any idea how difficult that would be? They are huge.'

Leo shuffled forward in the driver's seat, checked the road and then turned the van off onto the tarmac on the side of the road in silence. Switching off the engine, he twisted around in the narrow seat and stared hard into her face. 'I don't think that you have thought through the implications of what happens when the land is sold, Sara. That letter means what it says. The builders will need to clear the land before they start. Of course they will give you a chance to remove the greenhouses, but if you don't... They would be within their rights to demolish them.'

The blood seemed to drain from her face and she felt dizzy. 'Demolish,' she said in a weak voice. 'Could they do that?'

'Only if they had to,' he replied. 'But you have to be ready for that possibility.'

'I don't know if I'm up to this,' she whispered, her eyes fixed on the dusty floor of the van, which was littered with sweet papers, cat treats and random pieces of paper and other assorted rubbish. Which at that moment looked like a fair representation of how this week was turning out.

Leo reached across and took one of her hands in his. 'I don't expect you to do it on your own,' he said. 'There are great removal teams who could have you up and running in two or three days. The plants would never know the difference.'

He bent his head down so that he was looking up at her with a wide smile, warm and encouraging. And she was so glad that he was here holding her hand, helping her to get through this, that her throat tightened and she blinked away treacherous tears before squeezing his hand between her palms.

She was being so totally pathetic it was ridiculous! She was a grown woman.

'Laugh at me if you will, Leo, but Kingsmede Manor has been the one constant in my life for as long as I can remember and I just can't imagine growing orchids somewhere else. It's the only place I've ever felt loved and treasured and wanted. It's my safe place. That probably sounds ridiculous, but I mean it. Every word.

'I'm sorry,' she said, looking into those grey-blue eyes which were gazing at her with such compassion that she almost lost it. 'I know that you're trying to save my business and I appreciate that more than I can tell you. It's just that…everyone I have ever loved and cared about has gone and left me just when I needed them. I haven't seen my father since I was six, my mother is a ghost and then I lost my grandmother three years ago. That's why I came back to Kingsmede, because it belonged to my grandmother. And it would not be the same anywhere else. Does that make any sense to you at all?'

Leo looked into Sara's wide eyes, filled with concern, regret and love of the one place that she had made into her safe haven in this mad world, and his heart melted.

He stroked her short hair back over her ears, caressing the cropped layers as though they were made of the finest silk, his fingers moving from her temple in gentle circles while all the time all he wanted to do was gather her up into his arms and tell her that it was all going to be fine and that he could fix this for her.

That was his job after all, wasn't it? Fixing things for other people.

But he couldn't give her that comfort.

He had spent hours poring over the old designs for the Manor, sketching and drawing out elaborate schemes for wonderful glasshouses and a stunning conservatory, and enjoying every minute of it. Sara had searched everywhere for the more detailed schematics without success but he had already seen enough to visualise just how splendid the buildings could have been.

But the cold light of dawn brought with it the hard truth.

These designs were so elaborate that the cost of restoring the gardens would far outweigh the benefits to the hotel short-term. And he simply did not have any information to show that they would provide enough income during the winter to be worth the investment.

But it was more than that. If he proposed a garden restoration plan to the Rizzi Hotel group, it could put him at odds with the other plans he knew *would* work for the hotel. At odds with his aunt and his family at exactly the time when he was trying to impress them with how very clever he was.

Grand and fanciful concepts like garden restoration would expose him to the worst criticism of all from his grandfather—that he was being sentimental and putting people before the business.

No. That idea had to stay just that. An idea which would never be realised. He could not risk being humiliated by his grandfather. Not even for Sara.

While all the while this wonderful, courageous woman felt as though she had been abandoned by everyone she had cared for.

All he could do was open up his heart and share some of his own life in the vain hope that she would believe that there was someone in her life who knew how she was feeling and hurting. Then talk through real ideas which he knew would work for her.

'I do understand,' he said, 'more than you think. My parents passed away in a car accident when I was sixteen, but until then we used to live in a little house in the London suburbs. When you are a child you don't realise how hard it must have been for your parents, but my sister and I had a very happy childhood. I always knew that I was loved and wanted. We might not have had the latest electronic gizmo the other kids had, but they used to love to come to our house because it was always full of music and life and chatter.'

He smiled at Sara and tapped her on the end of her nose. 'Sometimes I have to drive through that part of town and I miss that old house. I was happy there.'

Sara gasped and slid her hand onto his wrist and held it there. 'I'm so sorry to hear about your parents,' she said. 'I can only imagine how awful it must have been for you. But I'm glad that you have such happy memories.' She smiled. 'Tell me about them. Tell me about your dad. What did he do?'

Leo took a breath. He had not been expecting that.

'My dad worked as an architect in a city firm, but his real passion was painting. I remember sneaking downstairs in the middle of the night so that I could watch him working frantically to cover the canvas with paint. Landscapes. Portraits. He could do anything. His fingers were moving so fast that they seemed to blur, and he was so wrapped up in the world that he was creating that he usually didn't even notice that I was there. It was his obsession.'

Then Leo's voice drifted away into a soft whisper that resonated inside the van. 'And then a few hours later he would put away his paints and put on his business suit and take a bus and then the underground to work in an office block with fluorescent tubes above his head, drawing up plans for more office blocks and car parks. And he did that year after year because he had a family he loved. I admired him for that sacrifice and I still admire him today.'

'He must have been a remarkable man,' Sara whispered, holding Leo's hand tightly.

Leo smiled and nodded, grateful for the rare opportunity to talk about the parents he had so adored and still missed on a daily basis and yet never spoke about to anyone, not even his sister or his aunt. 'They were both remarkable,' he replied.

He looked at her and his eyes sparkled with a fierce passion which was invigorating and almost frightening in its intensity. 'And that is why I am going to prove to my mother's family that she made the right decision when she chose to elope with my father. He was a terrific man and he loved her more than anything else in the world. Nobody disrespects him. Nobody. And that's why I need to show them that her son is worthy of that same respect.'

'What do you mean?' she asked in a low voice, calm and collected, trying to balance out the pressure and electrifying tension that crackled in the air between them.

'I've been invited to join my aunt for lunch at the Rizzi board meeting on Friday. She kept in touch with my mum from the day she walked out of the family home, and was there to take care of us after the accident. But she won't be there on her own—the whole family is coming up to Kingsmede Manor for the meeting, and that includes my grandfather, Paolo Rizzi. It is not going to be easy, but I am willing to take the first step to talk to him if he is prepared to listen in return.'

Leo's upper lip twitched. 'And I might just

show off a little about how successful my business has become. Or maybe a lot, depending on the reception I receive. I suppose that makes me a lesser person but this is a special occasion.'

'Of course.' She nodded slowly. 'Now I am beginning to get the picture. And I almost—almost—' she held up one hand as Leo opened his mouth to protest '—feel sorry for old Paolo. He won't know what's hit him. Good luck for Friday.'

Then she smiled and her voice dropped an octave. 'When are you going back to London?'

'Tomorrow. I need to catch up on my workload, but I'll be coming back here on Thursday evening. Why?'

'Oh, I was just thinking that I might be available for dinner on Thursday evening, Reg. Seeing as it will be your last night in Kingsmede before the big meeting. If the invitation is still open.'

'It would be my pleasure,' he murmured and reached out and took her hands in his as he stared deep into those green eyes, so full of hope and care.

'I want you to think about what I've suggested. You would still have your cottage and the main greenhouse at the Manor. That doesn't change. But your other two glasshouses would on the other side of the village. Would that really be so bad? You would still be Kingsmede Manor Orchids. Okay?'

'Yes…' she breathed out in a rush. '…I suppose I would. I will think about it. Thank you, Leo.'

The delight and fire of energy and enthusiasm in Sara's eyes burnt so brightly that Leo sucked in a breath of cooling air. If it meant so much to Sara to even suggest that there was a chance then he could give her a sprig of hope.

'Hey. We are a team, remember—Eloise and Reggie's Floral Specialities. Bring it on, Sara. Let's do this. Let's show them what Kingsmede Manor could have been. Ready to get started? We have a business plan to write.'

CHAPTER NINE

SARA stepped out of the shower, wiped away the condensation from the surface of the bathroom mirror and stared at herself through the hazy mist.

She was exhausted and it showed in the dark shadows under her eyes and the paleness of her skin. The plans for Tony Evans were complete. But even with Leo's help it had taken her twice as long as she had expected to photograph the orchids she had allocated to specific rooms in the hotel. She had eventually crashed into bed at two on Wednesday morning.

Leo was still working at the kitchen table when her eyes started to close and her head had started dropping onto her chest. She had a vague memory of his warm arms wrapped around her waist as he lifted her up and carried her in his arms the few steps to her bedroom.

Bliss.

She had only meant to nap for an hour or so;

when she woke Pasha was asleep on the bed and the morning was gone. And so was Leo.

She ran her hands through her short hair, pushing it back from her forehead, and wondered how she had managed without Leo all this time. She would never have achieved so much in the past few days without his help. She knew that, but of course it was more. A lot more.

Leo Grainger had come crashing deep into her life like a tsunami wiping away everything in its path and leaving behind a new world of… That was the difficult bit.

She felt so helpless.

Her hands clamped around the cool ceramic basin before she slapped cold water onto her face and patted it dry.

She should go back to the hot orchid house and check the humidity levels. The weather had changed from hot sunshine to the type of sticky cloudy day that threatened rain or even thunder. It was oppressive and so warm that she had slept without covers all night.

It was as though the whole world had changed from warm sunshine to cloud—not only the weather but in her heart.

How had she got herself into this position?

She had become so comfortable with her routine existence, but it had only taken one man like Leo Grainger to come wafting into her life in a vampire costume and it was as though the windows had been opened and a powerful light had illuminated a dark space, revealing what lay within.

And she did not like very much what she saw there.

Sara turned from side to side and looked at her naked body as objectively as she could in the misty mirror. On the surface she was the same girl she had always been. Tall, gawky, slim and without much cleavage to shout about.

It was as though time had turned back on itself and she was sixteen again, getting ready for her mother's birthday party. And knowing deep inside that she was never going to be pretty enough or glamorous and stylish enough to be the daughter her mother wanted and needed. Slick and shiny and well groomed were the kind of descriptions reserved for other girls.

How could a country duckling like her ever hope to be enough for a man like Leo Grainger? What had she got to offer him?

There was no future in their relationship, and it was ridiculous for her to even dream that there could be. Their lives were so very different in every way.

Did she really expect him to drive down to this village every weekend? And she could hardly go to London or fly out to some romantic hotel at a moment's notice without neglecting her customers and her nursery.

So where did that leave them?

Any idea that they had a future together was just a glorious illusion like the magical gardens described in the Victorian documents Leo had devoured with such pleasure the day before.

She felt Pasha purring and rubbing against her bare legs and she instantly reached down and lifted him up. Her grandmother's old cat didn't even struggle or try and scratch her once.

'This is the end of an era, Pasha,' she murmured into his warm dry fur. 'Things are going to be a lot different from now on. But we will be okay in the end.'

Except that, as Sara caught her reflection in the mirror, she could only see weary disappointment and finality in the sad eyes of the girl looking back at her.

And that shocked her more than she had thought possible.

Was this how it was going to be from now on? Not if she had anything to say about it.

'Well, Pasha, if this truly is the end of an era—' she smiled '—then let's make this a night to remember. Don't wait up. I might be quite late.'

Leo stared out over the hotel grounds in the late afternoon sunshine towards the fine filigree roof of the glasshouses on the other side of the lane. He knew that there was a small cottage there with a girl who made his heart sing and if he wanted he could walk over and be there in minutes.

But he wouldn't.

In a few short days Sara Fenchurch had become the only woman he liked to spend his time with. The person he needed to talk to first thing in the morning and last thing at night. They had spent hours chatting about nothing in particular and the time seemed to pass in seconds.

He liked Sara. He liked her a lot. And maybe, just maybe, he more than liked her. But that came with a price.

Tomorrow he would meet his aunt and the Rizzi family in what had been Sara's grandmother's dining room and give a presentation he had been thinking about for so long it had become a myth.

But instead of working every hour he could on the details he knew he would be challenged on, all he could think about was a pretty girl called Sara and the orchids she loved so passionately in this special world she had created for herself. A world so foreign to his normal life it could have been a distant country. And yet, driving back to Kingsmede that afternoon, he had felt almost excited about seeing the Manor again.

Which was ridiculous. He loved his life in London and the pulse and excitement of the city in his pristine, ordered workspace and home. She loved the cramped, hot and humid space between her rows of plants and a crazy, messy cottage.

The view of the Thames from his office on the fifteenth floor of the glass building in Docklands was worth every hour of relentless and unending conference work.

She loved the view of her flower beds from her kitchen window.

His triple layer electronic calendar was now completely full for the next five months and into the New Year. Her diary hung from a peg near the kitchen door and was just about to get a lot less crammed.

He should be excited about making the presentation tomorrow and relishing the thoughts of his triumph with the family. Instead of which he felt hollow and exhausted from the thought of leaving Kingsmede and Sara behind him.

He had changed.

She had changed his life.

She had given him so much—and what had he given her? His time, his opinions—but not the truth. He had not given her the truth. And she deserved better than that.

No matter what happened going forward, Sara deserved to hear the truth from him.

She would be hurt and probably angry to discover that he was a liar and a fraud. Other people had let her down in the past and now he was adding himself to the list.

Leo drew back the curtain and opened the bedroom window.

This was his last chance to spend time with Sara as the man she thought he was.

Time to make this evening something she could remember for the right reasons.

Sara tugged at the skirt of her fitted azure cocktail dress one more time before sucking in a breath, lifting her head and walking as calmly as she could into the reception area of Kingsmede Manor Hotel. Not as a delivery girl or wannabe orchid supplier, but as a bona fide member of the public here at the invitation of a very important guest of the hotel.

Tonight she was just a normal girl out on a date with a charming, handsome man who had invited her to be his dinner companion.

And just the thought of that gave her the jitters so badly that she almost slipped on the highly polished marble floor in her uncomfortable high heels which she had not worn for three years. It was a mystery how she had managed to wear shoes like this every day and blocked out the pain as the price of elegance. She truly was not the city girl she had once pretended to be. Not that she had ever been one at heart, she knew that now. Which made it even more incredible that Leo Grainger was even vaguely interested in her and wanted to spend his last evening alone with her.

Smiling to the receptionist who had given her a sly nod and wink of approval on the way in, Sara wrapped her fingers around her clutch bag as tight as she dared without destroying the poor thing to hide her nerves, and strolled casually over towards the hotel bar. She had only gone a few steps when the elevator doors opened and out emerged the man she had come to meet.

Leo was wearing a sky-blue shirt, highlighting his tanned skin and broad shoulders, and she had to fight back a sudden urge to throw herself at him and drag him into the elevator and shock the hotel staff. But of course she would never do that... She was still the Lady of the Manor as far as the locals were concerned. *Pity.*

'For once I am on time,' she said, her voice low and shaky. 'Nice shirt.'

Leo made a joke of glancing down at the shirt and flicking off an imaginary speck.

'Your timing is perfect,' he said in a voice of pure chocolate—hot mocha with extra marshmallows and whipped cream on top. 'And I thought you might appreciate a change from black. Just this once.'

'Then I am truly honoured,' she quipped with a tilt of her head. 'And you know it suits you.'

His reply was a slow laser-focused swivel of his eyes from her strappy summer sandals to the criss-cross of her one-shoulder cocktail dress. It was a look that would set any woman on fire and it was certainly working its magic on her.

She squirmed, and he knew that she was squirming, which made her even more self-conscious. This man was infuriating! His blue-grey eyes flashed with fire and light and her pulse grew hotter. At this rate she was going to need a shower before she ate dinner.

'You look sensational,' he whispered in a voice just loud enough that only she could hear it. 'And I missed your grand entrance. I don't suppose you could just pop outside and stride in again so I could enjoy seeing you in the wonderful dress. Just for me?'

She gave him a look which clearly answered his question. 'Ah, perhaps not. Maybe that is a good thing.' He grinned. 'I'm not entirely sure I could take it.' And he waggled his eyebrows up and down several times.

'Leo,' Sara said under her breath, and she looked from side to side to check that no one was listening to him, even though she was grinning with delight, 'behave yourself! This is a very respectable hotel.'

Leo instantly stood ramrod straight and saluted. 'Of course, my lady,' then gestured flamboyantly towards the elevator. 'Your carriage awaits, madam.'

Sara took tighter hold of the clutch bag as a nervous shiver ran across her back. 'Aren't we going to the bar for drinks before dinner?' she asked. *Or perhaps we are bypassing drinks and dinner completely and going straight to your bedroom? That would be nice.*

'For you, my lady, the public bar is not nearly good enough.' And then he smiled and presented her with the fingertips of his right hand as if he were handing her into a carriage, then seized upon her hand hungrily. 'It's right this way.' He tucked her hand tighter against his chest so that they were touching from thigh to shoulder as they glided into the beautifully polished elevator, which was just large enough for two.

She was so entranced by the delicious scent of this man she was pressed against that, when the elevator started on its upward journey, she jumped and flinched away from him, only to be pulled back by a firm hand against the middle of her back. Almost as if he was determined to keep her by his side for as long as possible.

With a lurching feeling of resignation and regret, Sara realised that this was the closest that she had been to this wonderful man since they had danced together and shared that wonderful moment on the terrace that Saturday evening, and was so taken back to that dance that she could almost hear their music playing in the background.

Then she blinked hard and stared in amazement at Leo.

'Is that a Viennese waltz that they are playing?' she asked in amazement. 'Elevator music has certainly improved around here.'

'I hope so,' he replied with a smile. 'It took all of my considerable charms to persuade the lovely receptionist to change the tape to one of my liking.'

He breathed the words into Sara's ear. 'It had to be our song. Nothing else will do.'

'Of course,' she said with twisted eyebrows, 'I totally agree,' and then her face relaxed. 'That was very thoughtful.'

'My pleasure.' He smiled and gave her one of those looks which were intended to entrance any female creature within one hundred miles' radius. He must have had advanced training. Because it was a total success.

Sara was still feeling bedraggled and dazed when the elevator doors slid open and she looked out onto what should be the third floor corridor to the guest rooms, if the elevator button was telling the truth. Then her brain connected with what she was looking at. That was crazy. There were no guest rooms on the third floor. The top of the house had always been the attic storage room and the servants' quarters—and her bedroom, of course, tucked away in the corner of the tower.

Her old bedroom. Oh, Leo.

A lump formed in her throat, so large she was in danger of never speaking again.

Leo slipped away from her side long enough to step outside the elevator, then turned back and stretched one hand towards her.

Sara looked out into the corridor over Leo's shoulder.

The electric lights had been turned off. And in their place were two rows of tall candelabras with a full complement of tall lit candles. The breeze from the elevator created a flickering wave of warm light that floated across the golden wooden floor towards them, warm with the aroma of beeswax and exotic perfume.

The candles were lighting their way down a narrow corridor and she instantly recognised where they were going, and it knocked her sideways that her suspicions had been confirmed.

This was the same piece of flooring that she had skipped and jumped and run down for so many years towards her old bedroom—the bedroom she had chosen as a child from every other room in the house.

'Shall we?' he murmured, and smiled at her with eyes transformed by the flickering candlelight into deep blue pools, and as she placed her fingers into the palm of his hand and stepped out of the elevator, she knew she had just taken a big step. She felt it in her heart and she knew it in her mind.

This was a journey she could not walk away from when Leo left her to go back to his life in the city. If she took one more step she would be resigned to a life of longing and missing Leo every minute that they were apart. A life of endless regret and emptiness until she could touch him and hold him and speak to him again.

It was a miracle that she had the strength to take that one step forward and clutch onto his fingers as though they were a lifeline being held out to a drowning woman.

His left arm rested lightly at her waist and he drew her to him as they strolled slowly down the narrow corridor in silence. It was probably only ten steps, but it was a journey she wished would never end.

Here in this carefully controlled space with Leo by her side, she felt contained and separate from the world and all the pressures and problems that lay outside both of them. With Leo she felt safe and sheltered and protected by someone who cared enough to go to all of this trouble because he knew that it would give her pleasure.

He would be an amazing lover.

It had been such a long time since anyone had actually done something so selfless for her and her heart swelled at the simple joy of it.

And she loved him for it.

She loved Leo Grainger.

It should have come as a surprise but it didn't. She had felt the world shift over these past few days as though tectonic plates were changing the shape of the continent that lay beneath her feet and underpinned her entire small world. She would not have it any other way, not when it felt this wonderful.

They slowed outside the wooden door she had once known as the gates to the secret world she had created for herself. But this time it was Leo who turned the handle and swung the door into the room and she gasped in delight and amazement at what she saw inside.

In contrast to the dim candlelit corridor, her

old bedroom was bright with late evening sunshine, which beamed through the stained glass
panels at the top of the open full-length windows.

Birdsong from the trees directly opposite
the window combined with the distinctive call
of peacocks on the lawns and a happy chatter
of guests on the floors below them to create a
soundtrack she had forgotten and yet was instantly familiar.

She closed her eyes and took in the special
aroma of old lavender sachets, wax polish and
dusty old wooden flooring and fixtures. It was
all there.

Blinking away tears of delight and pleasure
at being in this place again, she was aware that
Leo was standing by her side and he gave her a
small tug at the waist.

Where her bed used to be was a long sofa
and right in front of the window was a fine
marquetry table laid out for dinner for two with
the finest porcelain, silver cutlery and crystal
glassware. A bottle of very fine champagne was
chilling in a silver ice bucket. Waiting for her to
enjoy.

'I don't know what to say,' she managed to
squeak out, scarcely able to take in the beautiful
room.

'Then don't say anything,' he whispered,

standing behind her with his arms wrapped around her waist so that his chin rested on her shoulder and they could look out through the tall windows onto the trees, open countryside and her very own cottage and greenhouses below.

'I am just content that you like it.'

All that she could manage was a gentle nod of her head and she leant back against Leo's chest, allowing him to take her weight and revelling in the sensation of the strength of his arms around her and the warmth of his chest against her back.

'It's magical,' she finally managed to whisper in a hoarse voice. 'But how did you know that this was what I really wanted to see before everything changes?'

'Oh, that is quite simple,' he replied, the side of his head resting against hers. 'This is what I would have wanted if I had been in your position. Now, I think it's time for a beautiful lady to have some champagne and the finest food this hotel has to offer.'

She sniffed away a moment of intense embarrassment and pleasure. 'Yes, please, and seeing as you have gone to so much trouble, I might save some for you as well,' she murmured with a half smile, trying to be gentle and wanting so very desperately not to break the connection and the wonder of this moment.

And that really did make him chuckle, and his gentle laughter echoed around the room as she turned inside the circle of his arms and slowly lifted her hand so that she could stroke his cheek.

And then she kissed him. Her lips moved gently and smoothly across his so that, as his smile faded into surprised recognition, her fingers could move slowly to the back of his head, caressing his skin on the way. While all the time her lips were moving from the corner of his mouth over the warm and full bow of his lower lip and then taking possession of his entire mouth.

Leo's arms wrapped tightly around her back so that he was holding her completely against him, and this feeling of his hands on her dress, burning through the fine fabric against her skin, only added to the utter delight and heat of their heady kiss as he returned her passion step by step, touch by touch and sensual movement by movement.

She had never been kissed like this before in her life or shared and given herself so completely into the passion of the moment, but she so desperately wanted this man to know how she felt and the intensity of how much she wanted to be with him. She did not need champagne to fuel her intoxication—all that she truly needed was Leo and this moment in time. Everything else was extra and unnecessary.

Whatever happened in the future or even in the next day or two did not matter. All that mattered was that they were together and she could show him how much he had come to mean to her in only a few short but remarkable days when he had opened up the doors to show her what her new life could be like.

It was almost as if she was saying goodbye to this room, this house and the only way she could survive that was to have Leo by her side.

Nobody else in the world would do—ever again.

Breathless, panting with heat and the pressure of the blood pumping in her veins, Sara rested her forehead on Leo's chin, sensing his heart racing and his lungs drawing in cleansing breaths.

'Hello, beautiful lady,' he whispered, his eyes finding something totally fascinating in her hair, and holding her against him and caressing her with unbelievable gentleness and tenderness.

Sara revelled in the luxurious sensations that flooded through her body in slow languorous waves. Her senses seemed ultra tuned to every part of Leo. The soft fabric of his shirt against the warm skin that lay below, fragrant with expensive bath products blended with a subtle musk and aromatic perfume that was all his own.

She could feel powerful bands of muscle and sinew below the palms of her hands under his shirt. He was totally intoxicating.

'Can I see you again?' she murmured into his neck.

'Um?' he replied, but his mouth was too busy kissing her temple.

'I know that you are going back to London tomorrow, but I'd like to see you again. If you want to,' she blurted out in a rush, not wanting to break the connection but desperate for him to know how she felt. Suddenly the most important thing in the world was to make him hers.

'Look what you have done to me, Leo Grainger! I'm wearing dresses and heels and having romantic dinners. And I like it. I like it a lot. I need you in my life, Leo. Come back—tell me that you will come back and see me.'

His hand pressed her head deep into his chest and he embraced her with such love and tenderness, but she could hear the fast beat of his heart under her head, and his heavy breathing. And then the low sigh that was nothing to do with passion and deep feeling and everything to do with the bad news he was about to tell her.

Had she made a mistake? Had she totally misread him?

Sara lifted her head and looked at his face and

her grin faded. It was as though the blood had been drained from his skin.

'What is it, Leo? What's wrong? If you don't want me, just tell me.'

Sara reached forward to stroke his face, but Leo closed his fingers around her wrist and slowly, slowly, started stroking the back of her hand with the pad of his thumb.

'Oh, I do want you, very much, but there is something I have to tell you and it's not going to be easy for you to hear. There's no easy way of saying this, but I need you to understand that I had no idea how important it was for you to stay and work in the grounds of your old home.'

He took a breath and exhaled slowly before speaking again in a lower voice. 'You already know that the hotel chain want to redevelop the old gardens and build a spa extension to the hotel. What you don't know is that the designs for the spa are much larger than you might think, Sara. I've seen the plans, and the building work is going to extend across all of your kitchen gardens.'

She stared into his forehead and suddenly the realisation of what he was about to say hit her and hit her hard.

'Oh, no. No, Leo. Please tell me that they won't be building right next to the only greenhouse I will have left. The orchids need as much light and ventilation as I can get.'

He raised his blanched face and exhaled slowly before replying.

'I am so sorry, Sara, but the architect's plans have already been approved at the outline stage. The investment needs to use all of the space they have available to get the return they need, and that means building right up to the bottom of your garden. There will be glass—you can be sure of that. The architect wants to build a conservatory link between the house and the spa.'

'But that means they will be building over the foundations for the Orangery and the beautiful knot garden! Once that is under cement there's no going back. Oh, Leo, how do you feel about that after you've seen those original designs? Is there no way of changing their minds at this stage? And what about the old kitchen wall?'

'It will need to be totally demolished to make room for the new conservatory link.'

Demolished. The image was so Technicolor real she couldn't believe it wasn't happening at that moment, and her head started spinning, dizzy with the revelation. The fruit trees and the old orchard would be gone, swept away.

'I'm sorry. But this is not the end.' He smiled at her, squeezing her hand and making her look at him. 'I have given you other options, remember? I kept my part of the bargain, and I can help you find new property to rent. You can still have Kingsmede Heritage Orchids on the other side of the village. You did agree that was a possibility. Didn't you?'

'Yes, I suppose I did, but I was hoping that there was still a chance.' Her voice faded away and she caught hold of Leo's arms for support. 'When did you find out that the plans had been approved?'

'This morning. But you have to understand, I couldn't tell you about any of these ideas until I had spoken to my aunt. I was sworn to secrecy, Sara. I'm so sorry it turned out like this.'

'Secrecy? I don't understand. Why were you sworn to secrecy?'

Leo took a firmer grasp of her hands and his tongue moistened his lower lip in a nervous gesture which made the blood run cold in her veins without his need to say another word.

'You already know that my aunt is Arabella Rizzi. What I couldn't tell you was that she asked me to take an objective look at Kingsmede Manor and come up with some ways of increasing the profitability of the hotel. That's why I stayed here after Helen's party last Saturday. I was here on a secret project for the Rizzi Hotel chain.'

CHAPTER TEN

'OH, NO, Leo. No. *You couldn't do that to me.*'

'I was telling you the truth. Aunt Arabella asked me to take a look at the hotel and come up with a few ideas on how to turn it around and make sure it had a future. But she insisted that my reason for being here should be kept a secret. That was why I couldn't tell you.'

'I don't believe it,' Sara replied in a thin, tired voice. 'You were working for the hotel chain the whole time you've been here.'

And then her eyes closed. 'Of course. How stupid of me. All that talk about how much you loved design and architecture—it was all a lie, wasn't it? A carefully constructed plan so that you could persuade a foolish country girl to tell you everything you needed to know about the hotel so that you could feed it back to the family.'

Leo shook his head very gently from side to side. 'No, this was not a paying job—this was a personal favour to someone who means a lot to me. And I wanted to tell you, many times, but I gave my word that I would keep the real reason for my being here a secret. I am so sorry.'

'Did you know? Did you know that I was the only person who had access to those garden designs before you talked to me at the party last Saturday? I need to know.'

She scanned his face, desperate for him to deny it and fight back. But his full lips simply opened a little wider as though he was looking for words. But for once the lips she could kiss all day and never be satisfied were still.

'And I fell right into your trap, didn't I? I cannot believe that I actually showed you my own family photographs.' She looked up into his face and swallowed down hard. 'I have told you things about my family that only Helen and my mother know. Oh, Leo, I hope all this is worth it.'

Her lips were trembling so much Sara wondered that she could even form the words through the pain in her throat. Tears were streaming down her face.

'I thought you were better than that. I thought you were someone who knew their own worth and did not need validation from other people— it seems I was wrong about that too.'

He flung back his head and raised both hands

in the air, breaking away from her and stepping back, his face twisted into disbelief and resentment.

'Do you really think that I am so shallow that I would seek you out and pretend that I didn't know who you were, just to see what juicy bits of information I could use to impress my aunt? Are you serious? Do you truly believe that I would use you like that?'

'Yes,' she whispered. 'That is exactly what I think. You want to walk into your family party and score as many points as you can in the prestige status game and don't you dare try to deny it because I can see it in your face.'

She grasped onto the back of the nearest chair because her legs were wobbling so badly she thought she might collapse. Suddenly she was finding it hard to breathe. Her heart was begging him to convince her that she could not be more wrong.

'Sara! That was unfair. The spa is the best commercial option to make the hotel viable. Just as moving a few miles away and starting up again is your best option. Perhaps you are the one who was not willing to take the risk and move out of your comfort zone and your safe little cottage and get on with changing your life!'

His voice was sad and hard and bitter—and her voice sounded worse.

They were arguing, and she felt sick.

'I did take a risk. Leo. I took a risk on you! I trusted you, and you lied to me and you used me to get the information needed to impress your family. Is this what it comes to, Leo? Because if this is your world, I want nothing to do with it. Or you.'

'Now what? You plan to walk home? Sara! I'll take you back to the cottage if that's what you want. Stop being such an idiot! You can't afford to let some sentimental attachment to the past or to people come between you and your business decision. Trust me. I know. You have to put that all behind you now and move on.'

'Trust you?' She stared at him, her mouth slightly open. 'Yes, I have been an idiot. I was stupid enough to believe that you actually cared about me and wanted to help, and now I know the truth. And I am right back to where I always am. Unloved and alone, just when I thought someone cared about me enough not to walk away. Well, don't worry about tomorrow. You truly are a Rizzi—and in the worst possible way. Your grandfather will be very proud of you. Why shouldn't he? You are just as ruthless as he is.'

But, instead of facing her and answering her accusations, Leo turned and walked away from her, flung the windows open wide and stormed the few steps out onto the balcony; his power-ful muscular body that she had held against her, so tenderly warm only a few minutes earlier, now seemed as hard and as cold as the ancient stones.

And in an instant everything she had worked for over the past three years was blown away as dust and trampled underfoot.

All that sacrifice! All those exhausted, sleep-less nights she had spent worrying about not having the money in time.

And for what?

Her grandmother was gone—her dream lost for ever. And now she was about to lose the nursery and her heritage.

And where did that leave her?

'Thank you for your offer of help,' she whis-pered, 'but I need to do this on my own. You are going back to your life. So don't worry about me,' she whispered. 'You have such a bright future with your important family and that's all that matters, isn't it? Proving that you are worthy of their approval? Well, good luck with that. I'm sure they will love you for putting busi-ness before some foolish sentimental nonsense about people and heritage. Pity. I thought you actually had the courage to stand up for your-self… And for me, but it looks like I was wrong about that—wrong about a lot of things.'

Suddenly she stepped back and reached into her bag for the tiny package she had wrapped so carefully in tissue and ribbon and left it on the table next to their untouched meal.

'Thank you for your help, Mr Grainger. This is yours now. And I wish I had never kept it.'

Sara soaked in one final dose of the vision of his enchanting body, picked up her bag, turned her back on him and tried to leave. Only her feet refused to move and she felt dizzy and exhausted.

She could stay.

She could surrender to the need and admiration for all of the other wonderful and totally unexpected aspects that made Leo who he was. She could do that—and go right back to the girl she had been only a few days earlier when she went to the hotel to celebrate Helen's party.

So much had changed in her life since then. She should be grateful to Leo for helping her to change. Leo had made her stronger. And more determined than ever.

Simply the profile of him standing on the balcony in front of her with the sunset framing his head was a picture frozen in time that she knew would stay with her for ever. How ironic that it was her old bedroom in her old home. The old Sara would have jumped at him and apologised for being so silly.

No more.

'Goodbye, Leo. You got what you came for. I hope your meeting brings you happiness.'

He flinched once but did not turn and beg her forgiveness or ask her to stay. And she was not going to ask him.

She was tired of all the compromises she had made over the years to win the approval of people she cared about.

Which was why she silently took a grip on her clutch bag, gave him one final sideways glance, then turned her back on him and walked through the door and down the candlelit corridor towards the elevator which would carry her back to her life.

Some of the candles had blown out. Others were flickering in the breeze from the open door to her room.

If Leo Grainger truly needed her in his life then he was going to have to prove it was for the right reasons—or not at all.

CHAPTER ELEVEN

SARA yawned widely, jammed the telephone between her chin and her shoulder blade and started loading the collection of blush pink and cream orchids into protective sleeves inside the delivery crates she had dragged out of the rain into her potting shed office at some silly hour of the morning.

The sunny weather had changed during the long night into light showers. She had watched the droplets fall in the dawn light, refreshing the parched soil but not enough to top up her rainwater barrels.

'Did she say what shade of pink she was looking for?' Sara asked while struggling with a double-spiked plant. 'Hot pink or more of a pale pink?'

She stopped working, took control of the telephone and pressed her finger and thumb to the bridge of her nose. The florist was tearing her hair out at the number of times this bride's mother had changed her mind about the flowers only days before the ceremony. The orchids needed to be loaded into Mitzi and with the florist that morning or there would not be a bouquet or wedding flowers at all.

'Now calm down,' Sara said, trying not to panic or give in to the fact that she had only had two hours' sleep that night and most of that was in snatches of a few minutes at a time. 'I'm going to bring three shades of pink and plenty of the ivory with the pink centres just in case she goes back to the first idea and wants a single colour bouquet. Be with you in twenty minutes and we can sort it all out on Monday. No problem.'

No problem. Sara returned the phone to the charger, closed her eyes and dropped her head onto the surface of the desk, then realised that the pile of papers which usually cushioned the blow was missing.

Drat Leo Grainger for forcing her to clear up and file and sort and organize while they were searching for the garden designs. At this rate she might actually be able to find things and have desk space to work on.

Providing, of course, she had work to do at all. One medium-sized greenhouse was not enough to supply florists and hotels all through the year. Especially with the prospect of a huge spa building blocking out the natural light and ventilation, to say nothing of the view out of her kitchen window.

She sucked in a breath and sat back in her chair and let her head fall back.

Leo. He would probably be having his breakfast in the hotel now. No doubt planning his presentation which would knock the socks off the family who had failed him.

Oh, Leo. He had only been gone a few hours and she already missed him so much it was like a physical pain when she thought about it.

All during the long night she had half expected her doorbell to ring and his familiar face to be there, asking her to give him another chance.

Stupid girl. Just another way of punishing herself.

Her heart contracted at the mental picture she created in her mind of his strong lithe body dressed in nothing more than boxers, strolling around his hotel room like the male lion he was named after. Master of all he surveyed, proud and powerful.

She could walk over to the hotel in five minutes and be right back in his arms again.

She had done it again—she had handed over responsibility for her future to another person— and she had fallen into the same trap and the same habits, just like before. She had given her love and her trust to someone who was capable of destroying her in the simple act of walking away, taking her hopes and her dreams with him as he went.

Her dad, her ex-boyfriend and now Leo Grainger.

What made it even worse was that she had spent the night tossing and turning and thinking through everything Leo had told her about herself. And he had been right about so many things that it infuriated her.

It was her decision to hand power over to other people in the vain hope that it would buy their love and approval. Hers. Nobody else's.

She had worked so hard to do what they asked her to do and in the end it had not been enough. She had seen the pattern too late to save herself from letting her grandmother down, and she would never forgive her mother for that.

Sara's eyes fluttered open and she blinked away her tiredness and tears. The newspaper clipping on the wall seemed to mock her. Businesswoman of the Year? What a joke.

She was a joke.

She had turned into a silly girl who was trying to prove a point by staying on in this cottage when she could have stayed in London and found another job. Two other companies had offered her work and she could have moved overseas and made a life for herself in the sunshine. Her mother had even asked her to come and live with her after the funeral so that they could spend some time together. There was certainly enough room in her three bedroom apartment in a smart part of London.

Sara shook her head at the thought of her mother and her sharing the same all white kitchen and the oven which still had the instruction booklet inside because her mother had no plans to use it any time soon. Oh, no—her kitchen appliances were for show and certainly not intended to be soiled by food. Toast crumbs on her granite worktop were punished with fierce glares and the liberal use of kitchen paper.

Just like the artwork her mother collected which she did not like but had been told to invest in. The only genuine things in the whole apartment were the antique floral prints in her bedroom and the framed maps in the hall. The rest was modern abstract prints and…

Sara's head shot up and she banged the heel of her right hand several times against her forehead.

Of course! The entire hallway of her mother's apartment was decorated with architectural drawings and maps—and most of them were of Kingsmede Manor.

That was where the missing part of the garden design had to be. No doubt about it. She might have sold it to a specialist dealer but there was a chance that she had kept it. A small chance, but a chance all the same. The name of the designer was something she could show off with pride to her friends.

Sara glanced at her watch and gasped.

She had five hours to deliver the orchids to the florist, drive to London in her electric minivan, get to her mother's flat, find the drawings and garden plans she needed, persuade her mother to hand them over, then somehow get the plans to Leo before he could make his final presentation at the hotel over lunch.

Her hand paused over the desk telephone, then pulled back as she swallowed down a moment of fear and excitement.

What was she doing?

Leo did not want the plans. He had already made up his mind. This was his big chance to impress the family who had disowned his mother by showing them what a big tough professional businessman he was.

Turning up out of the blue at the Rizzi family board meeting would only embarrass him—and, knowing her luck, she would probably barge in with all sails flying just when they were congratulating themselves on welcoming Leo back into the family business because of his totally objective methods.

And humiliate and embarrass herself in the process.

Wouldn't that be a proud and special moment?

But what was the alternative? Sit here and wait for the axe to fall and the sound of bulldozers tearing through the walled garden? Or try and do something to make them change their plans before it was too late?

And then there was Leo.

Both of them had said things yesterday which could not be unsaid, and she was sorry for that, but he had been at fault. Of course he would never break his word to his aunt. But it still hurt to know that he had been working as a spy the whole time and said nothing.

And yet he was sincere when he told her that he loved the garden designs. She had recognised his passion and his interest.

This could be her only chance to give Leo an option to show what he could do. And let the family take him for the talented man that he was and not just some clone of his grandfather.

Um. Who was she to talk? She had her own family issues to sort out.

Straight back, chin up, she took a deep breath and dialled the number for her mother's apart-

ment. *Time to make the call she'd never thought
she would.*

'Hi, Mum? Oh—did I wake you?'

Sara glanced at her watch. Just after 7:00 a.m.
Ouch.

'Oh, yes, I'm fine. Sorry about that. I have
to be up early for the florists. Anyway, I won't
keep you long.' She gulped. 'Are you going to be
at home this morning, Mum? I need your help
with something and I'm afraid that it is very
urgent.'

Leo relaxed his shoulders and looked across the
antique coffee table at the smiling face of his
aunt and the disinterested glare of his grandfather.

Paolo Leonardo Rizzi was a stern, silent,
stocky man with short grey hair and an exqui-
site business suit who still held the power in
the Rizzi family hotel business. Except at that
moment he was looking rather uncomfortable
and out of place as he wriggled around a little
to find a dignified pose on one of the sumptuous
but overstuffed sofas that Kingsmede Manor
specialised in.

It had been Leo's aunt's idea to have a private
meeting for just the three of them in her suite
so that they would not be scowling at one other

from opposite ends of an imposing boardroom
table when they met after so many years.

So far, it had not been a total disaster.

His first meeting with this man who he had
last seen at his parents' funeral when he was a
boy had not been easy. Their initial handshake
had been guarded, almost as though his grandfather thought that it was beneath his dignity as
head of the family to give Leo his tacit approval.
And of course Paolo Rizzi had noticed that Leo
was wearing a fabulous diamond ring, a Rizzi
family heirloom, but was far too proud to do
anything but glance at it and then glare at Leo
through narrowed eyes.

Well, if that had been a tactic to intimidate
Leo—it had failed. Miserably.

A week ago Leo would have been infuriated
by that slight, but now he accepted it for what
it was. One person's opinion. He did not need
Paolo Rizzi's approval, but he would like it. And
that made all the difference.

His aunt had asked him to present his opinion—and that was what he was going to do. Leo
inhaled slowly. This was a tough audience but
he was used to that.

They did not need to know that he had worked
most of the night pulling together research and
background information to create two completely new designs.

Sara had been right.

He had tossed and turned for hours, going over and over in his mind what she had said to him: 'You are just as ruthless as he is,' before giving up and starting work on the plans that he wanted to present.

He had become the very person he despised. He had become his grandfather. So focused and driven by the need to succeed that he had lost his family and his ability to connect to real people like Sara. *And it had shocked him to the core.*

Shocked him so much that he decided to do something to prove that Leo Grainger was his father's son, not just Paolo Rizzi's grandson.

And now was the moment of truth. Time to find out if all of that hard work had been worth it and his family would appreciate his ideas.

His family. He could see some resemblance to his mother in his aunt, but his grandfather? Oh, yes, she was there. From the blue-grey eyes and strong handsome face to the broad shoulders and natural poise, this was probably what he was going to look like one day.

He could see where his mother had inherited her good looks from. And maybe the strength to stand alone and make her own path in the world. He could not have been prouder of his mother and the decision she'd taken to go against her imposing father.

And Sara. Sara was right here giving him that edge as well.

Perhaps that was why Leo sat back against the sofa cushions as though this was a friendly family gathering rather than a formal business meeting and was rewarded by a definite lift in his grandfather's eyebrows for a few seconds, until his aunt laughed at something Leo said and passed him more coffee before she spoke.

'I am so pleased that Leo was kind enough to take a few days out of his hectic schedule to give me a second opinion on the turnaround plans for Kingsmede Manor. I am really looking forward to hearing his ideas. So, over to you, Leo.'

'Thank you, Aunt Arabella. It was my pleasure. And my delight. Kingsmede Manor is a beautiful property with enormous potential.'

Leo passed two copies of the dossier of his plans across the coffee table. Only his grandfather sat in disinterested silence while his aunt dived in with chuckles of delight and amazement.

'I will leave you to read the detail about the two proposals on the table. The spa extension is a great idea but the design is too modern. After a few days at the hotel, I know one thing. It is the heritage and design history of the house which makes it unique. The Fenchurch family who built the Manor had stunning glasshouses, an orangery and a superb conservatory with the most amazing level of craftsmanship. We need to incorporate those elements in any spa design if we want to make this hotel so very special.'

He gestured towards the dossiers. 'You can see that I have added a conservatory-style link building between the main house and the spa and changed the spa layout to resemble more closely the original concepts.'

His aunt responded by waving the folder towards him with a nod. 'This is stunning, Leo. I cannot believe you came up with all of this work in a few days.'

'I can't claim all of the credit. At the turn of the century the owners hired a famous garden designer to landscape their grounds and create special glasshouses for the orchids they were passionate about. The designs in the second option came directly from that work. The orchid collection at Kingsmede Manor was so remarkable that they used to attract visitors from all over the country. Only a couple of the original orchid houses remain at the property but they are very special.'

'How special?' she replied, her eyebrows raised and eyes full of interest.

'Special enough for me to make some preliminary enquiries with orchid organisations around the world. The market potential for specialist holidays is huge—and that was only scratching the surface.'

His aunt shook her head and turned from page to page of photographs.

'I had no idea at all. Lady Fenchurch did not even mention this history of the Manor.'

'A huge pity. There is so much potential here. For example, I would also like to recommend that we commission the creation of a new orchid variety in honour of the hotel. The Kingsmede Manor Orchid would have elegance, class, heritage and style—but with a perfume that is totally irresistible. It would be unique and exclusive to the hotel and to this hotel chain and could create a powerful symbol for the brand.'

'An orchid? Well, that could certainly be very appealing to a niche clientele with discerning tastes.' His aunt smiled, but then a very masculine voice with a strong accent growled out from the other sofa.

'You must really care about this hotel very much to be so committed to the long-term future of this house and jeopardise your own reputation in the process? I thought Grainger Consulting were more professional than to engage in foolish sentimentality and connection to some vague idea of the past.'

Leo looked up at the most senior director on the Rizzi family board and one side of his mouth rose in a smile. 'I do love this house. I love everything about it, but most of all I admire the spirit of the place and those who have loved it and cared for it over the generations to make it the building it is today. I arrived here as a guest only a few days ago for the very first time, and since then I have fallen in love with it as any other guest will do. It is a unique place.'

He shuffled forward onto the edge of the sofa and leant towards Paolo Rizzi. 'I have spoken to one of the descendants of the late owner of the house and she has agreed to share the original designs for the gardens necessary to implement the restoration. If these plans go ahead this hotel will become one of the landmark boutique hotels in this part of England. What is more, a garden of this quality would attract gardeners and specialist groups to the hotel and create a perfect wedding setting and a luxury conference venue.'

Leo paused for dramatic effect before adding, 'Kingsmede Manor could be the gem in your hotel collection.'

Arabella inhaled deeply and gave a gentle nod. 'That is quite a claim. But I like the proposal, I like it a lot. Although I do have a question.'

Leo tilted his head towards his aunt even though he felt as though his grandfather's eyes were trying to burn a hole in the centre of his forehead.

'You said that *we* should commission an orchid. Was that simply a slip of the tongue or have I finally persuaded you to join the family business after all these years? Leo?'

He smiled back at her. 'Many years ago I took the decision to leave the hotel trade and go into direct business management.'

He shrugged casually, then strolled to the back of his aunt's sofa and rested one hand lightly on one of her shoulders and she immediately raised her hand and held his.

'It was a hard decision to make after all you have done for me. I would not be standing here now if it was not for the opportunity you gave me. And now I have another opportunity to do something remarkable for myself and this time it concerns my whole family.'

His grandfather lifted his head and frowned at Leo. 'What do you mean by that?' he said.

'Simply this. I do not want to spend the rest of my life trying to prove that I am worthy of being part of the Rizzi family. I know who I am and what I am capable of—but I think you

already know that. What you don't know is that
I have decided to sell my consultancy business
and retrain as an architect. It was the only thing
I wanted to do as a boy.'

He glanced from the puzzled expression of
his grandfather to the stunned face of his aunt.
'These past few days at Kingsmede have shown
me that I have a choice on how I live my life
going forward—and who I spend my life with.
It may take a while, but I would like to take the
time to get to know my Rizzi family. If they
want that.'

He smiled down at Arabella, who was looking up at him with tears in her eyes.

But, before anyone could answer, there was a
strange clanking noise from outside the window
and Leo glanced out to see a very familiar off-
white electric delivery van called Mitzi clatter
its way into the circular drive outside the Manor
and stop directly behind his grandfather's Bent-
ley.

The wheels had scarcely come to a halt before
the driver's door was flung open and a short-
haired girl in a bright yellow T-shirt and flower-
patterned capri pants jumped out and ran to the
back of the van.

Sara! What on earth was she doing here?

Leo shook his head and grinned. *The cavalry
had arrived.*

'You are so like your mother I cannot tell
you,' his aunt whispered with a glint in her eyes.

'Thank you. I take that as a very great com-
pliment,' Leo replied.

'You should. She was a remarkable woman I
was proud to call my daughter, and it looks like
she had a son with a good head on his shoulders.
Orchids.' His grandfather sniffed. 'Might work.
And it is a lot more interesting than another
boring swimming pool that nobody uses.'

And with one nod the decision was made.
'Let's do it. And you—' and he pointed one
finger at Leo '—I could use an architect on the
team. Come to see me when you're ready to
start that training. This is a family business, so
let's keep it that way.'

But, before he could say another word, the
door to the suite burst open and a slim brunette
staggered through with a huge picture in her
arms. It was so large that her fingers could
hardly stretch to grasp the ornate gilt edges and
it was in great danger of falling at any second.

'I found it,' Sara gasped as Leo took the
weight and lowered the map onto the table, then
gave a wave around the room. 'Hi everybody.'

'So I see.' He grinned in reply, then gestured
across the coffee table. 'Here is someone I
would like you both to meet. My friend Sara
Fenchurch used to live at Kingsmede Manor.'

And then he paused long enough to take Sara's hand. 'Sara is also the woman I am in love with. Who just happens to run the orchid nursery just across the lane.'

'Ah-ha. So this change of plan was not entirely business-driven after all?'

'The plan stands on its own merits, Grandfather. But yes, it was Sara who first told me about the remarkable garden designs which could make this house a unique tourist attraction. It was my decision to do more research into the profitability of a niche market. My recommendation stands. It's the right choice.'

'He is in love with me,' she said in a stunned voice as she grinned back at Leo. 'Well, fancy that. I suppose I have to marry him now and make an honest man of him. Good thing I am totally in love with you too, Leo. And I know the perfect wedding location.'

'Wait a minute. Are you asking me to marry you? In front of all my family?' Leo said, his mouth half-open in shock.

Sara nodded. 'Best way. My mother will be here in about an hour to make sure that you are the kind of man who is suitable for her daughter. Character references may be required. But, as far as I am concerned, you are the only man I could ever marry. The only man I want as my husband and the father of my children. And I am saying that in front of your family and proud to do so. Marry me, Leonardo Reginald. Marry me and make me the happiest woman alive!'

His answer was to gather her up into his arms, lifting her off her feet as they both laughed and squealed with happiness before Leo kissed her with such passion and love that they were both breathless and exhilarated when they came back down to earth.

There was a low growl from the sofa and Leo's grandfather heaved himself to his feet.

'I've seen and heard enough. Arabella, my dear. Let's find out if this hotel has any good champagne. I need a drink and it looks like this family has something to celebrate. It is about time.'

EPILOGUE

'AND for the second year running the award for Businesswoman of the Year goes to…Sara Grainger of Kingsmede Heritage Orchids!'

The ballroom of the prestigious London hotel exploded into a riot of cheering and wild applause and hoots of laughter.

Someone planted a kiss in the vague direction of her cheek and Sara knew that she was being hugged by someone fragrant—probably Arabella or her mother, but she was so bedazzled and dizzy from the flashing camera lights that she did not see who or where.

Blinking several times, Sara turned back to the table. Helen and Caspar, Leo and his aunt and her own mother were on their feet cheering and applauding and giddy with delight and love—so much love, she felt carried aloft to the podium and the smiling regional organiser who handed her the prestigious award.

'Many congratulations, Sara,' he said. 'The

judges were extremely impressed by your remarkable work on the restoration of the Kingsmede Manor gardens. How does it feel to know that your family's heritage will live on in such a wonderful way?'

Sara looked out across the sea of faces until she found Leo, who was smiling back at her with such pride and happiness that she thought her heart would burst with love enough to last a lifetime.

'I have enjoyed every minute of this project,' she replied. 'Grainger Consulting has put together a wonderful team of architects and garden designers. But we could not have done any of the work without the wonderful support of the Rizzi family and so many friends who have invested in the future of this remarkable hotel that I used to call home. This award belongs to them and the whole team and I'm so grateful for their passion and their time and the opportunity they gave me. Thank you all for making my dream a reality.'

The applause was still echoing around her as she made her way down from the platform in her stunning designer eveningwear until she was back in the embrace of the man who had made everything possible and the two families he had brought together.

Her husband, the trainee architect and garden designer.

And at that moment, as she smiled back at the man she loved, she was a winner all over again and could ask for no greater reward.

* * * * *